Avoiding Marriage

A PRACTICALLY MARRIED NOVELLA

KARIN BEERY

Cover Design: Hannah Linder

Published by Karin Beery, P.O. Box 31, Elk Rapids, MI 49629

ISBN: 978-1-969517-00-6 (Paperback)
978-1-952369-73-5 (eBook)

Contents

Endorsements

Karin Beery has crafted a novella that includes it all: pain, humor, romance, nerds, and—best of all—hope. A perfect read for a quiet afternoon.

~Mikal Dawn, author of the Emerald City Romance series and *A Holly Bolly Christmas*

Karin Beery must be a bit of a fiend to toss her characters into the messes they find themselves in, but it's always a blast to watch them battle their way out. Karin's is a truly unique voice in the world of contemporary Christian romance, and I'm already looking forward to her next release.

~Linda Yezak, author of Christian fiction with a Texas Twang

Full of heart and wit, Karin Beery has one of the most engaging voices in women's fiction. If you like stories of redemption, friendship, and hope with a nerd romance thrown in for good measure, you need to read this book!

~Katherine Karrol, Author of the Summit County Series

Dedication

For Norah Caverson, the original Smooch: Thanks for letting me borrow your nickname.

Prologue

Ashley Russell scrolled through Jessica Miller's LinkedIn profile again and second-guessed her husband's decision to marry her. Was there anything his ex hadn't accomplished? Bachelor's degree, master's degree, and two professional fraternities. A list of published articles. Membership in two service organizations.

Ashley shifted on the barstool, trying to get comfortable at the kitchen island. In theory it was a nice place to work—lots of sunlight, open space, and close proximity to the refrigerator and tea pot—but the stools clearly weren't designed for a woman's hips.

She opened a new tab on her browser as the back door swished open. The familiar thump of boots on linoleum made her smile. Her skin tingled as she anticipated her husband's hello.

Her husband. Four months after their wedding and the words still thrilled her. Her *husband*.

On cue, Russ stepped into view in the back hallway. He shrugged out of his tan Carhartt jacket and hung it beside the smaller Carhartt his mom had bought Ashley for Christmas. A necessity for life on the farm, her mother-in-law had said.

As soon as Russ stepped into the kitchen, he smiled at her. "This is my favorite part of the day."

"Dinner?"

"Funny." It only took him four steps to cross the kitchen and pull her into his arms. His beard tickled her face as he leaned down and kissed her neck. "How was your day, Mrs. Russell?"

"Busy." She adjusted the angle of her head so he could kiss her jaw. "The high school's tech program had a special graduation ceremony today. I took pictures for them."

"I'm sure they're fantastic."

"They're as good as they can be considering I took them under fluorescent lights in a yellow gymnasium."

Russ leaned back and looked her in the eye. "Is that bad?"

"It's not flattering."

"If you say so." Then he kissed her the same way he did every night when he came home from work and it still made her heart flutter. Or maybe it was her stomach. She couldn't put the conversation off any longer.

Pulling away, Ashley pressed a hand to Russ's chest. "Dinner's almost done. Will you make the salad while I check the roast?"

"Sure. Can we pick this up again after we eat?"

The hope in his voice made her laugh. "Yes, but first we need to talk."

Russ moaned as he walked toward the sink. "That's never good news."

"How can you say that?" She closed her laptop before checking on the roast. "There's a fifty-fifty chance that it's good news."

"Wrong. My sisters only tell me they want to talk when it's bad."

"Don't worry. It's not bad. It's just ..." How should she describe it? "Unexpected. And weird."

"Now I'm curious." Russ scrubbed his hands, then started on the salad. Ashley plated the roast and whisked up some gravy while the potatoes finished roasting. By the time dinner was on the table, a knot filled her stomach. If she wanted to eat anything, she needed to talk first.

She folded her hands on her lap and looked at Russ. "Did you know Jess graduated *summa cum laude* from Michigan State University with a degree in agriculture and natural businesses?"

He stopped mid-bite and raised his eyebrows. "You talked to my ex-girlfriend?"

"No. I looked at her LinkedIn profile."

"Why?"

Ashley sighed. "I feel stupid admitting this because I made such a big deal about it before, but I wondered if she might be a better fit to help in the farm office. I can help you with accounting basics, but I don't know anything about how the farm works. It'll take me years to learn."

He set down his fork and took her hand. "I was planning on keeping you around for a few decades at least."

"I know, but"—she pressed a hand to her stomach as she smiled—"I'm late."

"Late for what?"

"Really?" She leaned toward him. "Late for knowing I'm not pregnant."

His fingers tightened around hers. "Are you sure?"

"I haven't taken a test yet. I wanted you to be here when I did."

"But you think you are? How? Why? Couldn't you just be late?"

"Probably, but I've also been tired for the last couple of weeks, and I can't stand the taste of coffee right now."

Russ opened his mouth, then snapped it shut. After several uncertain seconds, he jumped to his feet and pulled her to him, burying his face in the hair at her neck. "You're going to have a baby."

"I still need to take a test."

"But you could be pregnant."

"I could be." Ashley couldn't stop smiling at the possibility of her own sweet baby. Her and Russ's baby. Which was why they needed to finish their conversation. "That's why I was researching Jess today."

Russ leaned away, but not before stealing a kiss. "What does Jess have to do with anything?"

"I want to keep learning as much as I can about the farm, but I'm already overwhelmed, between what you're teaching me and my photography internship. I know we haven't talked about it yet, but after the baby's born I ..."

"Want to stay home?"

Hope twirled in her chest. "How did you know?"

"That you would want to spend as much time as possible with your daughter?"

Ashley laughed. "We don't even know if I'm pregnant. Let's figure that out first, then we can worry about the gender."

"You need a daughter."

"Why?"

The lines of his face softened. "So you can carry on the legacy your mother passed along to you."

Her eyes pooled. "Don't say things like that. I'm already feeling weepy."

"I'll comfort you."

He leaned in for another kiss but Ashley stepped back. "We *have* to talk."

"About Jess?"

"Do you think she'd be interested in helping in the office?"

"Our farm's office? You want my ex-girlfriend to work with me?"

"No, I want an experienced, apparently brilliant, agriculture and business expert to work for us so we can focus on our family."

"And you'd be okay with that? Me seeing Jess every day?"

It was Ashley's turn to do the kissing. She wrapped her arms around her husband's neck and pressed her lips to his. It didn't take long for him to bury his fingers in her hair. She smiled against his lips. "Are you thinking about Jess?"

"Who?"

"Do you love me?"

"Yes."

"Is Jess really as smart as she seems?"

"Probably smarter."

"She already knows the family, she already knows the farm, and she already helped us with the college program. I know how highly you think of her, but I didn't think you'd consider hiring her if I didn't suggest it."

"You're right. I wouldn't have."

"But if you could pick anyone to help you run the office, who would it be?"

"Jess." His fingers flexed around her waist. "You're sure about this?"

"Yes, but let me talk to her."

Russ cupped Ashley's face in his hands. Her eyelids closed as his thumbs feathered across her lips and jaw. "You're amazing," he whispered. "Do you know that?"

"No, I just want to spend as much time with you as possible. If that means asking Jess to work in the office so you can come home to me"—she opened her eyes and kissed him—"then I'll give her the office." Russ's arm swept behind her legs, knocking her off balance and into his chest. She squealed, then laughed as he carried her through the living room toward the stairs. "What are you doing?"

"You have a pregnancy test to take."

Chapter One

J ess Miller counted another stack of bills as she endured another day of her self-induced yawn-worthy penance. "That's two hundred and fifty dollars, Mrs. Kent. Would you like me to deposit it all for you?"

The eighty-year-old woman shook her head. Not a strand of her blue-white hair moved. "I thought my math skills were better than that."

"It's not a problem. I can fill out a new deposit slip for you if you'd like." Jess picked up a blank deposit slip from the pile next to the withdrawal slips. Every slip in its place in her teller cubby at the Boyne Heights branch. Like every other branch of the bank, gray-green carpet covered the floors, matching the linoleum on every counter. Fluorescent lights and white walls created a cold, sterile environment that welcomed people in just long enough to do their banking without inviting them to stay too long.

Mrs. Kent chattered about her grandkids as Jess typed numbers into the computer. She processed the transaction and handed the woman her receipt. "Is there anything else I can do for you?"

"No, thank you. It's so good to see you back in town again. Say hello to your mother for me."

"When I see her." *If* Jess saw her.

"Jessica?"

She turned at the sound of her name, not that she needed to look. Her branch manager was the only one at work who called her by that name. "What can I do for you, Mrs. Lyle?"

Her former teacher turned banker rolled her eyes. "Amy. You're not in high school anymore."

"It's still weird."

Mrs. Ly ... er, Amy chuckled as she motioned toward her office. "Talk with me?"

Jess made sure her drawer was closed before making her way to Amy's office, the only space in the building with any warmth to it. Student artwork and family pictures covered the walls and desk. Jess moved an embroidered pillow from her chair to the other guest chair, careful not to let it fall to the floor.

Amy sat and faced Jess, clasping her hands on top of the desk and leaning across it. "Why are you here?"

"You asked me to follow you."

"Not in my office, at the bank. You didn't fill out the application for the branch manager job in Bellaire. Why not?"

Jess shrugged. "Who wants to move to Bellaire?"

Amy sighed. "Jessica, you are desperately overqualified to be a bank teller."

"I'm happy here."

"You're bored."

True. "But I'm near my family."

"Bellaire's not even an hour away. You could take the promotion and still see your family as often as you'd like." Amy cocked her head to the side. "What's really going on?"

"A lot." Too much. "I don't mind the work here. I'd rather work a boring job near Grandma Dot than commute for more pay and responsibility. I'm not sure if I'm ready for that yet."

"How's your grandma doing?"

"Better. The first year after Grandpa's death was hard."

"She's lucky she has you."

Maybe. Maybe not.

Someone knocked on the open door. "Jess? There's a woman here asking for you."

Jess leaned to the side to peek through the window wall. Ashley Russell? Why was she looking for Jess? Too many possibilities raced through her head. "I'll need a few more minutes."

Amy waved her off. "Go see what she wants. We can talk about this later if we need to."

Jess didn't need to, but she wasn't sure her boss would feel that way. Having been properly dismissed, however, she stood and smoothed out her gray pencil skirt before tugging at the cuffs of her white silk blouse. Just because her insides were a mess didn't mean she had to look it.

Pasting a smile onto her face, she stepped into the lobby. "Ashley, what a pleasant surprise." She offered her hand and Ashley shook it.

"I'm sure it's a surprise, but you don't have to pretend like it's pleasant. We're both adults. We can call this what it is."

Jess tried to pin down the right word. "Awkward?"

"That will work. I'd like to make it a little more awkward if I may. Can I take you to lunch?"

#

Jess scanned the menu again, but she couldn't concentrate on the words. The lunch crowd buzzed around her, filling the small building with their chatter. Ashley sat across from her reading her own menu. *Let's order first*, she'd said. Good thing Jess ate at this restaurant regularly—she already knew what was good.

Ashley set down her menu and waved at their waiter. "Might as well get started."

He smiled as he approached. "Are you ladies ready to order?"

Ashley motioned for Jess to go first. "I'll take the Cobb salad."

"Me too," Ashley said. "And an iced tea, please."

He took their menus and walked away. As he did, Jess summoned her courage. "How are you and Russ?"

"We're good. Getting used to being married."

The familiar tug of regret pulled at her, but she refused to give in to it. She could act as nonchalantly as Ashley. "How's the family?" That prompted a long sigh. "That bad?"

Ashley shook her head. "No, they're wonderful. There are just so many of them. It's a big change from spending my weekends at home alone."

"You're not close to your family?"

"It's just me and my aunt and uncle. They're both around eighty, and they live in Florida. I spent most of my adult life alone until last year."

Jess could only dream of that kind of space from her family. She'd heard that Ashley's parents had died when she was young, however, so Jess decided not to mention it. Instead, she asked, "Is that why you wanted to talk?"

"Sort of." Ashley took a deep breath and sat a little taller. "How do you feel about the Russell farm?"

Jess shrugged. "It's a good farm. I've never thought about my feelings toward it."

"I phrased that wrong. I meant to ask what you think of it overall. Is it profitable? Is it sustainable? What would you do differently if you had the chance?"

"I'm not sure how to answer that or what to answer first." A dozen different scenarios and questions came to mind. Jess asked the most urgent first. "Is the farm in trouble?"

"Not exactly, but we need help."

Jess's nerves switched on, ready for anything. "Please don't take this the wrong way, but why are you asking me about this?"

"I'm messing this all up. It was my idea, so I thought I should talk to you. Plus, I thought it might curtail any rumors."

"Rumors about what? What are you talking about?"

Ashley reached into her purse and pulled out a sheet of paper. "Russ put this together last night. It's everything that Tom used to do in the office."

Jess took the page. She probably could have created the document without Russ's input. She knew what it took to run the business side of a farm. Nothing on the list surprised her. "This looks accurate. Did you want me to review it to make sure you didn't miss anything?"

"No. Russ consulted with his uncle and Chad, so we know the job description is complete. We need someone to take the job. We were hoping you would."

"I'm sorry. What?" Jess stared at Ashley, waiting for the punchline. When Ashley raised her eyebrows, Jess shook her head.

Ashley chuckled. "I wish I'd had my phone ready to take a picture of your face just then."

"I'm sorry, this is just"—unexpected, bizarre, ridiculous—"surprising."

"I know. It surprised me too, but we need help, and it's more than I can learn in a year or two. I'm more of a liability than an asset. Russ says you're a genius about these things. I want him to have the best work partner possible, but I also want to make sure everyone's okay with the situation."

The one-two punch knocked Jess off balance. That Ashley would hire her husband's ex-girlfriend to make his life easier impressed her. The following insinuation, however, couldn't have stung more had it been a slap across the face. "I don't sleep with married men."

Ashley raised her hands. "I wasn't implying that you do. But I'm afraid it could be hard for you to see Russ every day if you still have feelings for him. I wouldn't want to put you in that position."

"You're worried about *me*?" No wonder Russ loved Ashley—talk about selfless.

"Russ thinks you're what's best for the farm, but neither of us is willing to sacrifice your sanity for it."

While Jess appreciated their thoughtfulness, she appreciated the offer even more. It was exactly what she needed—the chance to help everyone see that she hadn't always been an unreliable mess, even if she had to work with Russ and Ashley to prove it. "I'll do it."

Ashley's eyes widened. "I haven't even told you about the salary or hours. Don't you want to know all of the details?"

Jess traced her finger along the rim of her water glass. "Has Russ told you anything about my family?"

"Please don't take this personally, but we don't really talk about you."

She smiled. "You shouldn't, and for that I'm thankful. I won't bore you with the particulars, but let's just say that my family hasn't spent a lot of time thinking about what's best for me. The fact that you spent any time worrying about my welfare means more to me than any salary or benefits."

"I'm sorry to hear about your family."

She waved it off. "I'm used to it."

"That doesn't make it right."

Their salads arrived just in time because Jess was afraid she might jump across the table and hug Ashley. Russ had definitely made the right decision. If Jess were honest, she would have broken up with herself too. The months leading up to their breakup and immediately after had been the hardest months of her life, and she hadn't handled any of it well.

But now ... now she had a chance not only to redeem her reputation but also to get out of the bank and back on a farm. All she had to do was not blow it.

Again.

Chapter Two

Despite the brisk morning air, Jess turned up the air conditioner as she drove through town. The closer she got to the Russell farm, the warmer the car felt. She pressed her chest against the steering wheel to let her already sweating back cool off. Wasn't thirty years old too young for hot flashes? But it had to be hormonal. She didn't get nervous. Much.

Who was she kidding? Ever since she'd given the bank her notice, she'd slept less and less each night. Thank God for adrenaline.

As she drove out of Boyne Heights, orchards spread out for miles around her. Tiny green buds dotted long lines of cherry trees. Asparagus sprouts filled flat acres. Several dirty fields seemed empty, but within two months low rows of strawberry plants would fill them.

Jess not only recognized the plants in each field, she knew which families farmed them. The blessing and curse of still living in her small hometown.

Within minutes, she pulled into the parking lot of an unmarked cinderblock building, but she'd been to the farm office many times before. Four other vehicles sat in the parking lot, including Russ's work truck. Parking in the spot farthest from his, Jess turned off her car and took a deep breath.

"It's just a job. Your dream job. The best job you could ever hope for." She could handle expense reports, employees, and marketing. But could she handle Russ? With Ashley?

Only one way to find out.

No matter how uncomfortable this job might be, it had to be better than the tedium of teller work. Jess took two more deep breaths before picking up her purse and running to the office door before she could talk herself out of it.

She let herself in, expecting the same drab, functional atmosphere as before, but instead, lemon-yellow walls surrounded her. The same retro desks and chairs filled the space, but a fire-engine red couch filled most of the far wall. Someone with long brown hair lay on it with her back to the door. Ashley? A half dozen men stood in a circle eating donuts and talking. The place reminded Jess more of a kindergarten classroom than a farm office.

"Good morning." A deep voice pulled her attention from the primary-colored decor to the man walking toward her. Chad, Russ's brother-in-law, extended his hand. "Welcome back."

"Thanks." She tried to read his expression as they shook hands, but he wore the same half-smile he always wore. "There are more people here than I was expecting."

"That's my nephew, Carrie's oldest, and a friend of his." Chad pointed over his shoulder, but he was so tall that Jess had to peek around him. "We'll see how they do this summer."

It wasn't hard to figure out which two he was talking about. The teens were nearly as tall as the other men, but only half as wide. Teens on a farm didn't surprise her, though. It was the two men in crisp jeans, button-down shirts, and clean shoes that stood out. She was pretty sure the shorter one styled his dark, wavy hair. "Who are they?"

"They're from Central Northern Michigan College. They're here about that program you set up."

She huffed. "I reviewed a proposal and made some recommendations. Russ did the rest." She nodded toward the couch. "What about that? Should we try to be quiet?"

Chad shook his head. "She sleeps like a rock."

"But why's she sleeping here?"

"She's been coming in every day to get the office ready for you. She usually takes a nap in the afternoon. She's early today."

"Is that normal?"

"It is for a pregnant woman."

The ground shifted, or maybe it was just Jess's world that moved. Russ was going to be a dad? "She didn't mention it."

"They haven't told anyone, not even me. It's an educated guess."

"Rachel slept a lot when she was pregnant?"

"*Is* pregnant." The half-smile widened until it filled Chad's face. "Four and five are due next month."

The couch creaked. Jess turned in time to see Ashley push herself up as a mass of hair fell into her eyes. When she pushed it back, she blushed. "Sorry about that." She pulled her hair back into a knot and grinned at Jess. "It's good to see you again."

Jess nodded, not trusting her voice. She tried to make eye contact, but her gaze went to Ashley's midsection. The mother-to-be stood and tapped her husband's shoulder. They spoke quietly, then he waved Jess over.

"Jess Miller, this is Ted Richardson from CNMC. He's our contact for the work-study program, which starts next year. This summer we're going to work out the details."

She shook hands with the taller, blonder man. "Nice to meet you."

"This is Carter Palmer. He's a historian."

"Genealogist."

"What's the difference?" Jess asked.

"I focus on people, not events."

"You study dead people?"

He smiled, crinkling the skin at the corners of his dark blue eyes. "I study and preserve the past."

"I'm the farm manager." She offered her hand. His callus-free handshake was surprisingly firm. "I'm not sure if I can help you with anything, but I will if I can."

"I'm really just here to see how this program works so I can propose a similar venture for the history department."

"You teach history?"

"I do."

Jess smirked. "So, you're a historian."

He laughed. "I guess technically I am, but my hope is to focus more on the genealogy of the area."

"The dead people. Got it." Before he could argue, she looked at Russ while pointing at the wall. "What happened here?"

"That would be my wife." Most people wouldn't notice the tightness at the edge of Russ's lips, but Jess had studied that face—and those lips—for years. He was fighting a smile.

Ashley rolled her eyes as she raised her arms in surrender. "Yes, I did this, but it's not my fault. The man at the hardware store basically admitted that he mixed the wrong colors. I wanted to brighten the place up. Not turn it into a—"

"Banana," Russ and Chad said together.

"I'll repaint it after I find a better color."

The front door opened, and Chad's three sons paraded in, followed by the most pregnant woman Jess had ever seen. She forced her jaw shut as Rachel shuffled inside. "Sorry to interrupt. I need to pee."

"Rach." Chad shook his head, but he rushed to his wife's side and offered his arm.

She swatted it away. "I have ten pounds of *your* offspring inside of me boxing with my bladder. Is there really anyone here who doesn't understand that pregnant women pee a lot?" She scanned the faces in the room, pausing at Ted and Carter. "I don't even know you, but I'm sure you understand."

"Anyway," Russ said, turning his attention back to business, but Jess couldn't pull her gaze away from Rachel and Chad. She'd always admired their relationship and had secretly hoped she and Russ would end up like them.

Despite her earlier announcement, Rachel didn't rush to the bathroom. Instead, she stopped to hug Ashley, who winced. Rachel gasped as she leaned back. Ashley's eyes widened. Rachel hugged her again, wrapping her arms completely around Ashley's upper back. She winced again.

"Are you serious?" Rachel stepped back and smacked her brother on the arm as she smiled at Ashley.

"Ouch. Am I serious about what?"

Rachel looked at her husband. "Did you know?"

"I've had my suspicions."

Russ crossed his arms. "Suspicions about *what*?"

Rachel clapped her hands. "You're pregnant!"

All of the Russells started talking at once. Rachel and Ashley got teary. Jess stepped around everyone in an attempt to give them as much privacy as the already crowded office would allow. She made her way to the kitchenette and the coffee pot, where Carter offered her his steaming mug.

"No, thanks." She wanted to distract herself from the celebration, but Ted's phone rang, so he stepped outside, leaving her with the historian. Jess sighed as she leaned against the counter and waited for the family to calm down.

"I wasn't expecting so much excitement this morning," Carter said.

"I wish I could say it's not always like this, but you never know what to expect with the Russells. This could be a once-a-week occurrence."

"You've worked here for a while?"

She shook her head. "It's my first day, but I've known them for years."

"Quite the first day."

He had no idea.

Chapter Three

J ess stretched her stiff neck and shoulders. The computer screen blurred in front of her. "I'm ready to call it a day."

On the other side of the desk, Ted checked his watch. "Wow. We've been at this for five hours."

"I should have been paying attention. I don't like to sit for so long, but"—she waved her hand over the still-cluttered desk—"things are usually more organized than this."

"Did you know it was going to be this bad when you agreed to the job?"

"I didn't know exactly what I was getting into, but I've known Russ for years, so I'm not surprised."

The man on the couch—Carter, was it?—stood. "You certainly seemed to enjoy all of this."

"What makes you say that?" Had she given off some kind of vibe?

He motioned toward her purse. "Your phone's been dinging for the past half an hour. You didn't even notice."

If only. She wouldn't tell him that she'd given her family members their own special ringtones so she knew when they were calling ... so she could ignore them. Instead she said, "I do enjoy my work. Which is a good thing because I should probably take some of this home with me." With Ted around, she'd finished less than half of what she'd hoped to accomplish. It was going to take a lot of work to get the office organized and the college program up and running.

She'd just picked up a stack of folders when Carter appeared beside her. "I'll carry those for you." He smiled as he slid the paperwork out of her hands.

"I, uh ... okay." She forced herself not to sigh. It wasn't an overly large stack of papers, but she was pretty sure his assistance had less to do with chivalry and more to do with wanting her phone number. Men had been carrying things, opening doors, and coming to her rescue ever since she'd developed curves. That was one of the reasons she'd fallen so hard for Russ—he was always more impressed with her brains than her bottom. She'd have to let Carter down easy.

"Do we need to lock up?" he asked as they all gathered their things.

Jess shook her head. "Russ is still out in the orchard. He'll stop in before he goes home." She made her way to the door with Carter behind her.

"I thought this was your first day on the job," he said.

"The family and I go way back. I know a lot about how they run this place."

"Then maybe you can help me. Earlier, when the family was here, I heard someone mention Tom. I haven't met him yet, have I?"

How to broach that subject? They stepped outside and into the brisk evening air. The days were already getting longer, and Jess was ready for summer. She'd take as much sunshine as she could get.

Her phone beeped again. She could use it as an excuse to avoid Carter's question, but that would only delay the inevitable and force her into a familial conversation in front of a stranger. No, she needed to be honest with her would-be beau. Let him see what went on behind her blonde waves.

Stopping mid-parking lot, she faced the college professor. "Tom was Russ's cousin and business partner. He died in a freak hiking accident, but not before proposing to Ashley. He was a crack businessman, but a bit of a social flake, so he didn't tell anyone about her. She showed up here not knowing he was dead, and no one knew who she was. The next thing anyone knew, she and Russ were engaged."

"Wow."

"It gets better. Russ and I used to date, but I had a meltdown, and he dumped me. A few times, actually. I didn't learn my lesson, though, so I showed up at his house after I found out about the engagement. Thankfully, he's a forgiving man and Ashley seems to be some kind of saint, so now I'm here—working for my ex-boyfriend and his new, pregnant bride to fill in the void left by his deceased cousin." She took the folders from him as he stared at her, eyes wide. With a satisfied smile, she headed to her car. "Do you still want my number?"

"I wasn't going to ask for it, but I'll take it if you're offering."

Jess spun around to see if he was serious. The idiot smiled.

"Carter!" Ted waved at them from beside a car on the other side of the parking lot.

"He's not going to wait for you to write it down, so I'll tell you what"—Carter reached into his back pocket and took out his wallet, then pulled out a business card—"here's *my* number. Call me if you ever need to vent. I'm a great listener." Before she could argue, he jogged away.

What had just happened? Shifting the folders, she held up the card.

Carter Palmer. Associate Professor. Board Certified Genealogist, National Society of Genealogy.

Wow. The hot professor was a nerd. Of course, she herself didn't look like the train wreck her life had become, so who was she to judge anyone on appearances? She wasn't really sure what she'd call him about, but Gran might get a kick out of knowing a genealogist, so Jess kept the card.

Her phone rang again.

With everyone else gone, there was no reason to avoid the calls any longer. Stuffing everything into her backseat, she checked the screen. Her brother. That call could go either way. "Hey, Felix. What's up?"

"Gran's trying to get ahold of you."

"I know. I've been working." She slid into her car and started the engine. "You didn't really need to call me for that. I can check my messages."

"I know. I wanted to see how close you are to home. I need a ride."

Jess's body tensed as she pulled out of the parking lot and steered her car toward home. "Where to?"

"It's been a rough day. I could really use a meeting. There's one—"

"At the senior center in half an hour." She floored the gas pedal. She knew the time and location of every AA and NA meeting within a fifty-mile radius. "I'll be home in ten. That should give you plenty of time to get there."

He sighed, his relief practically pulsing through the phone. "Thanks, Jess."

"Anything for you." Anything to get her big brother back. "I'll see you soon."

As promised, Jess stepped into her parents' house—well, her dad's house—ten minutes later. Felix stood by the door. He took the keys, kissed her cheek, then ran outside. She said a silent prayer that he'd get what he needed from the meeting. They'd been helping him for the past six months. His sponsor had recently celebrated ten years of sobriety. Jess hoped and prayed her brother would be as lucky.

"Is that you, Smooch?"

"Hi, Dad." After hanging her coat and purse on the coatrack, she padded across the worn hardwood floors to the family room. Her dad sat in his recliner, still wearing jeans and a logoed work shirt. Some car show played on the television. Instead of beer, he took a long pull of ginger ale. His friends in the electricians' union had given him a hard time about giving up alcohol until he'd told them about Felix's problem. Her brother had told their dad that it wasn't necessary to give up anything for him, but they hadn't had alcohol in the house since Felix finally checked himself into rehab. Jess had never actually heard her dad tell her brother he was proud of him, but each case of Vernors said it for him.

She kissed her dad's head before dropping onto the couch and propping her feet on the antique chest turned coffee table. "Have you talked to Gran today?"

He shook his head. "I just got home. My cell died on the job, otherwise Felix could've reached me and I would have let him take my truck. You shouldn't have rushed home."

"I was on my way. What do you want for dinner?"

"I can make my own meals."

"I know you can, but I live here too. There's no reason for both of us to cook—and that's not an excuse for you to get fast food every night."

"Last week I got Subway. You said that's healthy."

Jess rolled her eyes. "I said it's healthy-*er*. That doesn't mean you should eat it every day."

"Eh, I wouldn't want to." He took another sip of soda before his eyes widened. "You know what I could go for?"

"Chili, tacos, or spaghetti?"

"Tacos. How'd you know?"

"You have a limited flavor palate."

"It's not limited. It's refined."

Jess laughed. "Down to your three favorite foods."

"That's all a man needs in life."

"I think there's ground beef and salsa in the fridge."

She started to stand, but her dad stopped her with a hand on her arm. "I can brown meat. You call Gran. I'll cook dinner."

"You don't have to. I can—"

"I know you can, Smooch, but you worked a full day too. You can make spaghetti tomorrow."

Before she could argue, he disappeared into the kitchen. A few seconds later, the gas stove ignited. Taking her cue, she muted the car show, then dialed her grandmother. While the phone rang, Jess's gaze settled on the family photo above the television. It had been almost two years since her mother left and Dad still wouldn't take down that stupid picture.

"Hello?"

"Hi, Gran. It's Jess."

"Jessica, sweetie. Are you okay? I've been calling you all afternoon."

"I'm fine. I was at work, that's all. Are you okay? You called me six times. If it's an emergency you can call Felix. You know that, right?"

"Of course I do." Her soft voice stiffened. "Your grandad had dementia, not me."

Jess smiled. "I wasn't implying that you do. I just wanted to make sure you have his number."

"It's on my phone list, but I need to go to the store and he doesn't have a car yet."

"What do you need?"

"My favorite lipstick broke, and I only have one box of tissues left."

"And?" She waited for the rest of the emergency.

"And what?"

Jess massaged her temple. "That's all you need to buy?"

"That I know of, but once we get to the pharmacy, I may need some more items. One never knows."

Jess tried not to let her frustration show. "Can your lipstick wait a day or two? I just got home from work. Dad's cooking and Felix went to a meeting."

"Oh." Something shuffled. "Of course."

Gran meant it, but Jess heard the disappointment—the loneliness—in her voice. Not wanting to contribute to that disappointment, Jess asked the one question she knew would make Gran smile, even if it made her cringe. "Have you heard from Mom?"

"I did. She sent a lovely postcard from Maine last week."

"Wasn't she in Vermont last month? Why'd she leave?"

"Why don't you call her and ask?"

"If she wanted me to know where she was, she'd call me. Or Felix. Or Dad." Her voice cracked on the last word. She sucked in a less-than-calming breath. "Why don't I pick you up tomorrow and take you to dinner, then we can go shopping?"

"I'd love that. Your grandad used to take me out for dinner and shopping every week. We did that for fifty-six years."

Jess's heart cracked. "He loved watching you try on all of those silly outfits."

"Stylish, sweetie. There's never an excuse not to be stylish."

She didn't have the heart to tell Gran she hadn't been stylish since the 1990s. Instead, she said, "I'll see you tomorrow."

"Wear something nice. There's a new nurse here I'd like you to meet. He's tall and enjoys cooking."

Fabulous.

Chapter Four

Jess sighed as she closed another folder. How had Tom successfully run the farm for so long with such bizarre bookkeeping skills? No doubt it was a testimony to the family and the farm's history that they continued to succeed despite no discernable organizational structure. She'd been at it for two weeks and still couldn't figure out his system. At least she was almost done reading everything. If she wanted to get through the rest of the files before the end of the day—and she wanted to—she would need another cup of coffee. Or maybe six.

Alone in the farm office, her boots clicked across the cement floor as she made her way to the coffee maker. She was dumping in the last scoop of grounds when the front door swept open.

"Sorry I'm late." Ashley rushed into the room with a purse slung over one shoulder and paper shopping bags in both hands. She blew at the hair hanging in her face. "Did I miss anything?"

Looking around to make sure she was the only one in the room Ashley could be talking to, Jess said, "I don't think so. Was I expecting you?"

"Maybe not. Did I know you were going to be here today?"

"I work here now. I plan on being here every day. Should I not be here?" She'd never considered that. Maybe remote working would be best.

Ashley waved her off, then unpacked the bags. Two cans of paint, a bag of potato chips, oranges, pretzels, cookies, string cheese, pudding cups, and masking tape. "I hope you don't mind if I do some work while I'm here. I get bored at the house by myself all day. My mind's been so scattered lately that I can't remember what I have and haven't told Russ. I'm sorry if I forgot to tell you I'd be here."

"It's your farm. You don't have to explain anything to me." Jess would've expected that declaration to sting, but it didn't.

Ashley sat at Chad's desk and ripped open the bag of chips. "You're the manager. You should know what's going on. I don't want anything to surprise you." She offered the bag to Jess. It was only ten o'clock, so she shook her head. Ashley grabbed a handful of chips. "I don't want this to be weird, but I'm not sure how to make it so it's not weird."

"Me neither." That confession actually helped Jess relax. Rolling another desk chair across the room, she sat beside Ashley and picked up the pretzels. "I'd offer you some coffee, but it's caffeinated."

Ashley's entire body sagged. "I'd love some coffee. Do you know how hard it is to find a good-tasing decaf?"

"Nope. Besides the caffeine withdrawals, are you feeling all right?"

"Most of the time, but some days I feel completely unhinged." She motioned at the food. "Thus the selection of food. I never know what I'm going to want or when I'll want it, so I try to be prepared. It wouldn't be so bad if I could control the cravings, but last week I started crying when I couldn't find anything chewy in the house."

Jess tried not to smile.

Ashley snorted. "Go ahead and laugh at me. Russ did."

"He didn't!"

"He did, which made me cry harder. Long story short, I now have shelves for crunchy, creamy, salty, sweet, chewy, soft, hard, and sour foods. And pizza. He filled the freezer with almost a dozen different types of frozen pizza."

"He's a good man." That truth stung, but not as much as it used to. That surprised her.

"How's your grandma?"

The surprised her even more. "My grandma?"

"Russ said you two are close. He also said your grandpa died not long before you broke up. I imagine that was hard for her."

Jess could practically feel Grandad's arms around her as she recalled her last visit with him at the hospital. "Gran's adjusting. She's visually impaired, so my grandad used to drive her everywhere. He was always the helper. It surprised us all when he got sick so suddenly. He was dead in less than a month."

"I'm so sorry."

"Thank you."

"And your grandma?"

Regret clamped around Jess's chest. "She moved into a home."

Ashley reached over and squeezed her hand. "I'm *so* sorry."

"I really didn't want to like you, but you're making it hard." She hadn't meant to admit that out loud. Would she ever stop embarrassing herself?

Ashley smiled. "The feeling's mutual."

"I'm not a threat. I promise."

"I know, but it's hard not to worry with Wonder Woman working in the office."

Warmth coursed through Jess's cheeks. "Wonder Woman?"

"Have you read your resume? Looked in the mirror? Don't be so modest—and eat your pretzels." She looked at Jess's slim midsection and glared. "Maybe have some pudding cups too."

Not wanting to upset her pregnant boss, Jess ripped open a chocolate pudding cup and dipped a pretzel into it.

Ashley gasped. "You *are* a genius." She opened her own cup and scooped the pudding out with a chip. She popped it into her mouth and moaned.

Jess smiled. She couldn't remember the last time she'd had fun with a girlfriend. Of course it would have to be with Russ's wife. Could life get any weirder?

Chapter Five

Jess laid her cards out on the table. "Gin."

"That's impossible." Gran leaned forward, the extra skin on her arms squishing between the tabletop and her blue-and-white striped sailor shirt. "How can one person win six hands in a row? I'm telling you, that's not possible."

The grandfather clock in the care home's cafeteria chimed four times. "We've got an hour before dinner. You have plenty of time to redeem yourself."

Gran tossed her cards on the table and shook her head. "I can't handle any more disappointment today."

"Who else is disappointing you?"

"The manager. Costs are going up at the farm"—Gran's name for Brookside Assisted Living—"so I'm losing some of my luxuries."

As she gathered the cards, Jess looked around the traditionally furnished facility. Four-top laminate tables surrounded by mauve-colored chairs. Pastel flowered wallpaper. Thin, high-traffic carpet. The building also included an activity room/gymnasium, large living room-type area with a fireplace, armchairs, and couches, and private sitting areas throughout the halls. Gran's apartment, like most of the others, included a kitchenette and bedroom big enough for a queen bed. The clean, friendly, functional facility had everything Gran needed—and she'd picked it out herself—but it wasn't over-the-top.

"What luxuries are you losing?" Jess asked.

"They've decided to go à la carte with their services. Cable and internet aren't included anymore, so I'll have to pay more if I want those in my apartment. I can use the TV in the living room, but I don't want to watch *Jeopardy* every night. The new season of *The Bachelor* starts in four weeks, and it's Seth from last season's *The Bachelorette*." She pressed a hand to her stiff white curls, as if anything besides gale force winds could move her expertly styled hair. "That boy reminds me of your Grandad. I hope he finds a nice young girl. He was too good for that Kiersten."

Jess laughed, but her humor didn't last. "How much are they charging you for cable?"

Gran shrugged. "It doesn't matter. I don't have the extra money. The doctor wants me to try a different blood pressure medication and the co-pay's more expensive. I'll just have to wait my turn in the computer lab and find out what happens the day after."

"I don't think you have a computer lab."

Gran pointed down the far hallway. "Someone donated old laptops. They'll be slow, but at least I can check up on Seth. Later this afternoon, a nice young man will be here to give us lessons."

Internal alarms sounded the same way they did every time Gran uttered the words *nice young man*.

"He's very sweet. A real computer whiz. Owns his own company and has three dogs."

"Gran—"

Gran pushed her chair back, then brushed the wrinkles out of her white slacks. "I know. You don't need help, but that doesn't mean I can't keep my eyes open. Now, I need to use the powder room. I'll be right back."

As Gran walked away, Jess pushed aside thoughts of the computer whiz and pulled out her phone to scroll through her emails. How had she missed the news about the care home? She searched back for a week and couldn't find anything. Leaving her purse on the table to reserve their space, she made her way to the front desk.

Lois, one of the regular volunteers, smiled at her as she approached. "How are you today, Jess? Keeping Dorothy in line?"

"I'm not sure I have the power to do that, but I'm killing it at cards today."

"Good. She gets cocky when she wins all the time."

She didn't need to tell Jess that—Gran was the one who'd taught her to trash talk. "While we were playing, she mentioned something about the changes to her rent and services here. I didn't get an email about that. Could you forward it to me and double-check that you have my correct contact info?"

"Sure." Lois hit a few keys on the keyboard in front of her, then frowned. "It looks like your name has been removed as Dorothy's contact."

"What? Who would do that?" And why?

"You know I can only share information with people who are listed as contacts." Lois leaned forward and whispered, "It would be against our policy to share private information with anyone who isn't in the system. Unless your name's Dorothy or ... *Angela*, I can't tell you anything."

Jess braced herself against the faux marble counter.

Lois stood and placed her hand over Jess's. "Are you okay? Your face is white."

"I'm fine." Or she would be, as soon as she talked to her traitorous grandmother.

"Jessica, sweetie, you shouldn't leave your purse on the table." Gran joined her at the desk and held out her purse. "Not that anyone here could outrun you with it."

She glared at Gran. "Like Angela?"

The old traitor turned around. "Have you seen Al? I wanted to introduce you. He's very nice. Doesn't smoke."

"Nice try." She took Gran's arm and headed toward her apartment. "We need to talk." Jess ignored her grandmother's protests and the polite nods and questioning looks from passersby. She didn't know what to say or how to say it, but as soon as she shut the apartment door, she couldn't stop the words. "How could you do that? *Why* would you do that? Is Angela in town? Have you talked to her? You need to take her off your contact list and put me back on. Today."

"Don't call her Angela. She's your mother." Gran poured herself a glass of iced tea before shuffling to the small living room and sinking into her favorite green armchair. "Which question would you like me to answer first?"

"I don't care because none of it matters. She left us—all of us—and you're going to take her name off your contact list and put me back on."

"Jessica Grace Miller, if you want to have this conversation you will not talk to me like I'm a child."

Jess dropped onto the couch across from her grandma. The late afternoon sun filled the cozy room with warmth and light, but Jess couldn't appreciate it. Not with a no-account mother on the loose. "Tell me what happened."

"Why don't you get yourself some tea first?"

"No, thank you."

She sighed. "Fine, but don't interrupt. Angela has been checking in every month since she left. I know you won't talk to her, but she loves you and she wants to know how you're doing."

Jess huffed.

Gran raised her eyebrows.

"Sorry."

"I don't tell her everything, of course, but I did tell her when you moved back to town. She didn't want you to feel like you had to take care of me, so we decided to take some of the stress off you and let her help me with the farm."

Jess slouched against the couch and closed her eyes as another layer of stress poured itself over her already burdened shoulders. "I appreciate the thought, Gran, but having you cut me out of your life and hoping that Angela shows up when you need her isn't going to make my life easier. How do you know she can take care of you?"

"Don't be silly. Your mom raised you and Felix just fine."

"Are you serious?" Jess laughed as she looked at Gran. "Felix is a drug addict and I had a nervous breakdown at thirty."

"Jessica—"

"Where was she when you decided to move in here? Did she sort through boxes with you? Cry with you?" Tears filled Gran's eyes. Jess mentally punched herself. "I'm sorry. I didn't mean to ..." What? Tell the truth?

"I don't know what I did wrong," Gran said. "I love your mother, and I taught her right and wrong."

Jess moved to her grandma's chair and sat on the arm. She wrapped her arm around Gran's shoulders. "You didn't do anything wrong. Something inside her just snapped when Grandad died." The same way something inside Jess had snapped when her mom left. Her stomach churned. Were they really that similar?

"Maybe I could have helped you or Felix more."

"Unless you had strapped on hockey pads and gotten between Felix and that skate blade, there's nothing you could have done for him. It was literally an accident. None of us ever thought he'd get hooked on the painkillers."

Gran leaned into Jess and sighed. "We're a bit of a mess, aren't we?"

"We sure are."

"I hope it doesn't take too long to clean us up."

So did Jess.

Chapter Six

J ess closed the drawer and smiled. It had taken three weeks, but she'd finally filed the last piece of paperwork. It wouldn't have been possible without Ashley's initial efforts to sort through and organize everything. She might not know a lot about farming, but she clearly had a head for organization. Jess needed to thank her for that help. She'd add that to her list of things to do.

She refilled her coffee cup and was sitting back down at her desk when the front door opened. A petite pregnant woman waddled into the office. Despite her nearly overpowering stomach, her crisp blue capris, lacy maternity top, and red kitten heels made Jess uncomfortably aware of her own jean shorts and Michigan State University t-shirt as she stood to greet her. "Can I help you?"

"I'm Dr. Amelia Davis from Central Northern Michigan College. I'm looking for Carter Palmer."

Did he work here now? "I haven't seen him for a few days."

"I'm a little early. I'm sure he'll be here." Dr. Davis rubbed her lower back. "Do you mind if I sit down?"

"Not at all. I hear the couch is comfortable."

"If I sit there, I'll never get out. This is fine," she said, pulling out a desk chair. "I'm at that fun stage of pregnancy where I'm uncomfortable if I sit too long and I ache if I stand too long."

"I've never been pregnant, so I'll take your word for it."

Dr. Davis smiled. "It doesn't matter what you hear. No two pregnancies are the same. This is my third, and each one has been different."

Jess tried not to stare at the woman she'd originally assumed was in her mid-twenties. A mother of three *and* clearly some type of professor? "You don't look old enough."

Amelia smiled. "It's nice to hear that now, but it was frustrating in college when everyone thought I was fifteen. On my twenty-first birthday, I had two bars refuse to serve me because they assumed my license was fake."

The door opened again, and Russ and Chad stomped in, leaving piles of dirt by the front door.

Jess motioned toward their guest. "Russ, Chad, this is Dr. Amelia Davis. She's from CNMC, and she's here to meet Carter."

Russ faced Chad. "I thought we were working with Ted. Who's Carter?"

"He's from the history department," Amelia said. "I'm the head of the department. We're here to work on a possible genealogy work-study program, similar to what the business department is doing."

Russ looked at Jess, his face tense. "You can handle this?"

"Of course."

He smiled, releasing his own tension and some of Jess's. "Perfect."

The door opened again. "Sorry I'm late." Carter rushed in but stopped two steps inside. "I didn't think we'd draw a crowd."

"Don't mind us." Russ motioned toward Chad's desk. "We're just grabbing some info, then we're out of here."

Carter made eye contact with Jess. Next to Russ's and Chad's Carhartts and dirty boots, he stood out in his crisp, dark jeans and gray sweater over a collared shirt. He smiled at her and her stomach flipped. "I wasn't expecting the office to be so crowded. Can you recommend somewhere for Dr. Davis and me to meet?"

"Sure." Jess moved an extra chair to her desk, which was the furthest away from Chad's. "You two can sit here. I can take my laptop to the couch."

"Are you sure?"

"Absolutely." She pointed to where Russ and Chad were already pulling out invoices and jotting down notes. "They're the opposite of ADD. Once their attention is on something, it would take a minor explosion to pull it away."

Carter set his messenger bag on the floor beside her desk. "So this isn't the time to ask Russ questions about his family?"

"Not anything important. Besides, if you want to know anything about the Russells, you need to talk to Kathleen. She's the history buff."

His eyes brightened. "Kathleen Russell, president of the Boyne Heights Historical Society and Museum?"

"You know her?"

"No, but I want to. I was going to ask if they're related."

"She's Russ's mom."

"It looks like you may have picked the right family, Mr. Palmer." Amelia shuffled across the room and sank onto the nearest chair. "Now, what else do you have to show me?"

Jess didn't want to eavesdrop, so she slipped her laptop off the desk and made her way to the red couch. As she sank into the firm yet squishy seat, she held in a sigh. No wonder Ashley liked to nap in the office. The couch was amazing!

As Jess's fingers clacked across the keyboard, she tried to focus on her work, but Carter's rich voice kept snagging her attention. Somehow he made words like *heirloom* and *inventory* sound interesting. An hour later, Russ and Chad were gone and Jess had only written two emails, but she'd also started a list of people, places, and things that might help Carter with his program. Not that she had a lot of experience with anything historical or genealogical. Was that even a word?

Amelia groaned as she stood. "It sounds like you have everything under control here. If you'll excuse me now, I think it's time to head to the hospital."

"What?" Jess and Carter jumped to their feet in unison.

"You can't drive," Jess said. "I'll take you."

The doctor laughed. "My husband's in the car. He hasn't let me drive myself anywhere in days. I appreciate your concern and your offer though. Mr. Palmer, I'll need your full syllabus and an outline of supplemental materials and proposed community partnerships to present to the trustees next month."

Amelia and Carter spoke quietly to each other as he escorted her out the door. That gave Jess a few minutes to figure out how to present her information without it being obvious that she'd listened to their conversation instead of working. Would he think that was helpful, or creepy? She probably should have thought about that before eavesdropping, but it was too late now. Might as well be helpful. She'd just sat back down in her desk chair when Carter, Chad, and Russ returned to the office.

"I don't think I'd want my wife to work until she went into labor," Carter said. "I don't even know Dr. Davis that well and I'm worried for her."

Chad laughed. "Rachel took it easy with our first son, but I couldn't get her to stop for the rest of them. Not even with the twins. I've offered to hire a nanny for the last month of her pregnancy but she doesn't want anything to do with it."

"I don't even want to think about it," Russ said, rubbing a hand across his face. "Ashley's probably going to try to take pictures of her own delivery. I'm already trying to figure out how to hide her camera."

They continued to tease and bemoan each other's situations as Jess tapped her foot and checked the clock. While she waited, she typed up a few more ideas on her laptop. A few ideas turned into a paragraph, which turned into a page.

"Am I interrupting?"

Startled, Jess spun around, losing her balance and kicking out to steady herself.

Carter grabbed his shin and winced. "I can take a hint."

"I'm sorry. I was actually waiting for you to finish with the guys. I must have gotten distracted." Jess hopped up and offered him the chair. "I can get you some ice."

"It's not that bad, I promise." He smiled, pushing her chair back toward her as he pulled another chair beside it. "What were you working on?"

Warmth crawled up her neck and cheeks, but she wasn't about to let an hour's worth of work go to waste. "I couldn't help overhearing what you and Amelia were talking about. Honestly, I don't understand your fascination with all of the ancestry stuff, but I've lived here long enough that I think I can help."

"Amelia?"

That was her name, wasn't it? "Dr. Davis?"

He laughed. "Sorry, I don't think I've ever heard anyone refer to her by just her first name."

Jess blushed. "I should probably call her Dr. Davis too."

"I don't think she'll mind, but I'm sure she'd be curious about what kind of help a business genius can offer the history department."

Anxiety thickened Jess's throat, but she pressed on. "It sounds like you need connections, right?"

"That's the goal. The more families and museums I contact, the better my chances of finding the right partners."

"How many partners do you need?"

"I'm not sure yet. I'd like to set things up with a few different farms or museums so we can rotate the curriculum every year."

She scribbled some notes for herself and reviewed her list. "Between me and my grandma, we can get you the names of all the original families."

"Original families?"

"The original settlers." She pointed to her list. "There were four families that settled here in the 1850s, and my gran knows all of them. Not the settlers, I mean, but their descendants. There's a lot of oral history that hasn't been recorded yet, but there's also a lot structural history, if that's a thing. Is it? What I mean is there are still some original buildings. I was thinking—" She looked up and paused. Carter sat across from her with his forearms on his knees and a smile filling his face. She swallowed past her nerves. "What?"

"Look at you, getting excited about dead people."

She rolled her eyes. "I'm just saying that I've lived here most of my life, and Gran has spent her entire life in Boyne Heights. We know who you should and shouldn't talk to. You might not know that Marilyn Beals isn't the family historian, even though she's the one who still lives on the farm. It's actually her sister Cora who kept all of the family records and photos. She took a lot of it with her into the care home, but she knows it can't stay there. I have that kind of insider information. I can help you."

"Not that I don't appreciate it, but why?"

His blue eyes seemed even bluer against his gray sweater and dark, wavy hair as he stared at her intently. She didn't really have a good reason. She could lie, but she wasn't sure she could come up with a convincing one. Instead, she shrugged.

He cocked his head to the side. "That's it?"

"I don't know what to tell you. I heard you talking and it got my wheels turning. I don't know how to do this sort of thing, but I know where you can get the info you need. It's just not in me not to help if I can." When he didn't respond, she crossed her arms. "You don't like that explanation?"

"It's fine. I was just wondering what it would take to get you interested in all of these dead people."

She laughed. "Good luck with that."

"That sounds like a challenge."

"A declaration of truth."

"We'll see." He swung his chair next to hers so they were sitting beside each other facing the desk. When they were that close, Jess realized how broad his seemingly narrow shoulders really were. Unlike most of the men she worked with, who smelled like plants, dirt, or fertilizer, Carter's scent reminded her of the beach—fresh and crisp.

When he faced her, their noses were inches apart. "Now," he said, "what have you got for me?"

She picked up her list, intent on the mission, not the man. She had a farm to run and a reputation to fix. She didn't have time for history nerds, no matter good-looking or good-smelling.

He tapped the list. "You've been busy. This is going to save me hours of work."

And probably distract her for as many. What had she been thinking?

Chapter Seven

"You made it!" Kathleen Russell stood on the wraparound porch wearing a pale blue tracksuit and waving as if greeting a long-lost friend. She squinted against the noontime sun and smiled.

Jess hoped her smile didn't look as confused as she felt as she parked in front of the quintessential farmhouse—two stories, the porch, black shutters against white siding, and a red barn to the side.

She hadn't even unbuckled her seatbelt before the driver's door opened. "Jessica, it's wonderful to see you again."

"Hello, Kathleen." As soon as Jess was out of the car, Kathleen pulled her into a hug. The warmth and familiarity of it tightened her chest, but she doubted it was from the strength of the hugger. "I appreciate the invitation, though I'm surprised to meet you at Russ's house."

"It's closer to town and I have errands to run later, so it made sense to meet here."

It didn't, actually, but Jess didn't mention it. Instead, she followed Russ's mother through the house into the kitchen. Russ and Ashley sat at the island staring at her, a bowl of popcorn in front of them.

"Hi." She waved.

"Hi." Russ looked at the calendar. "Do we have a meeting? Did I know you were coming over?"

"I thought so."

They all faced Kathleen just as the doorbell rang. "I'll get it." She stepped back through the living room and disappeared.

"What's she up to?" Jess asked, not really sure she wanted to know the answer.

Russ shrugged. "We'll find out soon."

"Thank you, Mrs. Russell. You have a lovely home."

Jess recognized that dark chocolate voice, as rich and tempting as the nerd it belonged to. Carter froze in the doorway when he spotted everyone. "Once again, I didn't realize this was a group event."

"Mom?" Russ crossed his arms.

Ashley looked at her husband. Then at Carter. Then at Jess. Carter, then Jess. Carter and Jess.

No! "Kathleen?"

Carter raised a finger. "I feel like I missed something."

"Welcome to my life," Russ said. "And my house."

"Your house?"

"Don't overreact." Kathleen swatted Russ on the arm. "Carter came down from Petoskey. Your house is closer. He drove so far, the least I could do was meet him partway."

"Yeah. His twenty-minute drive must have been brutal."

"Stop it. I thought it might be nice for you two to spend some time together. You could use another friend."

Russ's face turned fire-engine red as Jess tried not to laugh out loud.

Ashley snorted, then coughed. Her husband glared at her.

Carter smiled. "That was very thoughtful of you, Kathleen."

Russ pointed a finger at him. "Don't encourage her. She's a world-class busybody and she knows it."

"I do." Kathleen beamed. "Now, everyone sit down so we can talk."

"About what?" Russ asked, but he took Ashley's hand and led her to the kitchen table.

Jess waited for Carter, then followed the processional. The Russells sat on one side while Jess and Carter took the other.

"Carter contacted me about the Boyne Heights Historical Society and Museum," Kathleen said. "He wants to work for me."

"I'd like to work *with* you," he said as he sat. "CNMC is interested in setting up another hands-on program like you're doing with the business and agriculture departments."

Russ's eyes widened. "Why would you want to work with the museum? Have you seen it?"

"Only online, but I'm excited to get in there."

"Isn't it exciting?" Kathleen set mugs of coffee in front of everyone. "We could teach the students how to handle and preserve documents, research local ancestry, and even curate exhibits."

Jess pressed her lips together. She'd seen the museum's exhibits. She wouldn't exactly call them "curated."

"I need to work with local organizations to develop the hands-on portion of the curriculum," Carter said, looking at Russ. "When I saw Kathleen's name on the museum's website, I figured you might be related and thought I'd drop your name."

Russ rolled his eyes. "Because I have so much pull with the museum crowd."

"His plan obviously worked because here we are." Kathleen brought the cream and sugar over, and they spent the next several minutes personalizing their coffee before she finally sat. "Jess suggested Carter call me, so I thought she should join us as well."

"I appreciate the thought, but I don't know anything about this stuff."

Carter nudged her. "You gave me some good leads."

"And you know all about the farms." Kathleen looked at her watch and gasped. "Oh, no! I forgot what day it is. I have a lunch appointment in Traverse City that I can't miss. Do you mind if we reschedule? I can meet you in Petoskey."

Russ rolled his eyes again.

Carter waved off Kathleen's offer. "That's not necessary. I'll come back down. We'll just need to make sure your schedule's open."

"You are a wonderful young man. Go ahead and email me the information you need. I'll make sure to have everything ready for you the next time." She kissed him on the cheek, then walked around the table and kissed Russ. "I like your new friend. You should invite him over for dinner sometime."

"Mom." Russ sighed.

"I brought over some steaks, but I'm not sure when I'll be back. Maybe you could enjoy them without me. Jessica, you should stay and have mine."

Subtle. Jess wondered if Kathleen had talked with Gran recently.

"You'd better go so you don't miss your meeting." Russ pushed his mom away from the table. "Have fun."

Ashley rubbed her husband's back. "This all feels so familiar."

"What does?" Carter looked back and forth between them all.

As soon as the front door closed, Russ turned his attention to Carter. "I'm sorry. She doesn't know when to stop interfering. She used to stick with family, but I guess she's branching out."

"I really don't know what you're talking about. What am I missing?"

Heat scorched Jess's cheeks. "We're being set up."

"Don't sound so glum." Ashley nudged Russ. "Her last match worked. Besides, you guys are great. It could be worse."

Carter raised an eyebrow. "You barely know me."

"I don't know you at all, but I know how to search social media."

Russ crossed his arms. "Why were you looking for him on social media?"

"I had to. When your mother told me he was coming over—"

"You knew?"

Her neck turned red. "I had my suspicions."

"This isn't happening." Jess looked at Carter. "I'm sorry you got sucked into my nightmare."

"I don't think getting set up with me is a nightmare."

"You're missing the point."

"So *you're* the nightmare."

Jess's jaw dropped as her hackles rose. "I am *not* a nightmare."

Carter shrugged. "You've already told me what a wreck your life is."

Her hackles wilted. "It is a wreck. That's why I don't have time for a setup."

Ashley snorted. "That's a weak argument."

"Maybe for you, but I don't need to give anyone else around here another reason to talk about me."

Carter leaned toward her. "Who's talking, and why do we care?"

"I'm trying to repair the damage I've caused, to my reputation and my family's. I don't want people thinking I'm such a lost cause that I need my ex-boyfriend's mother setting me up with the first available guy she finds. No offense."

"None taken," Carter said.

Russ laughed. "You've got it wrong. If Mom's interfering, it's not because she thinks you're incapable. It's because she cares and she wants you to be happy. Well, that's what she's told me for years. I think it's true."

"But why me?" Carter raised his hand. "None of you know anything about me."

"You asked my mom about the museum. Next to her family, that's the most important thing in her life. She spent hours a day there after my dad died, and something about it helped her move on. Don't be surprised if she wants to adopt you later."

"I think *my* mom might have something to say about that."

Wouldn't most moms? Except maybe Jess's.

Ashley leaned back and honed in on Carter. "So ... you have a mom. You might as well tell us everything else now. It'll save us the trouble of having to investigate you."

"She's already corrupted you." Russ shook his head. "I'm going to need food for this."

Jess considered escaping, but it wasn't like she had anything else planned for the day. Instead, she turned her chair so she could see Carter better.

He raised his hands in surrender. "I'm thirty-five years old and an associate history professor at CNMC."

"What does that mean?" Ashley asked.

"It means I'm not quite as well known or well educated as a full professor."

"How much education do you have?"

"I have bachelor's degrees in history and organizational leadership with a master's in public history from Middle Tennessee State University. I've been accepted to the history PhD program at the University of Michigan, and I'm an accredited genealogist with the International Commission for the Accreditation of Professional Genealogists."

Jess tried to keep the surprise off her face.

"What does that look mean?" he asked.

Obviously she'd failed. She shrugged it off. "You're incredibly educated. And a bit of a nerd."

"Says the woman with a degree in agriculture and natural resources, as well as a master's degree in agricultural, food, and resource economics from Michigan State University."

How did he know that?

"I didn't know you had a master's degree," Russ said as he set a plate of pastries on the table. "When did that happen?"

When all eyes turned to Jess, she focused on straightening her blouse. "Last year. I haven't really used it since then so there was no reason to talk about it."

"What'd you write your thesis on?"

"The stability and management implications of supplying marginal land for bioenergy production in northern Michigan."

"Using farm waste as your fuel supply?" Russ asked.

"In some of the studies."

Ashley raised her hand. "What does that mean?"

Jess smiled. "In a nutshell, I wanted to see if it would be possible for farms to use some of their waste products to create renewable energy for themselves and even their communities. If that's possible, it can help them support themselves in years when crops are small or ruined. There's a lot more to it than that, but that's the elevator pitch."

Carter snickered. "And you think I'm the nerd."

Ashley raised her hand again. "We've established that you're both very smart, and kind of nerdy, but I still have questions."

He nodded. "Ask away."

Ashley bit into a pecan roll. "Eva been mahwied?"

"No."

"Engaged?"

"No."

"Kids?"

"No. I believe there's a proper order for that, so I won't be having kids until after the engagement and marriage."

Jess leaned toward him. "And what if you fall for a woman who already has kids?"

"Insta-family. Why? Do you have kids?"

Russ spewed coffee across the table as Ashley choked. Jess was sure the heat in her face would singe the hair off her head.

Carter winked. "What else do you have?"

Jess narrowed her gaze. "Family?"

"Mom, high school history teacher. Dad, high school English teacher. Younger brother, high school civics and government teacher."

"Why aren't *you* a high school teacher?" she asked.

"Too educated."

"Snob."

"I'm not a snob, it's the truth. I got my master's immediately after I finished my bachelor's degrees, so I couldn't get a teaching job because I was overqualified. Technically I'm underqualified to teach at CNMC, but they accepted my application since I'm already enrolled in a PhD program." The soft consonants and his relaxed speech almost made his bragging sound lyrical.

"You have an accent. Where are you from?"

"Tennessee."

She grimaced. "Isn't it hot and muggy there?"

"About like it is here in the summer, which is one of the reasons I wanted to move here. It reminds me of home, but I also get to ski and snowshoe."

"Have you gone to Bear River Valley yet? That's one of my favorite places to cross-country ski."

"I don't think so."

"You'd know if you'd been there." Jess smiled just thinking about the corridors of naked trees opening up to acres of gleaming, undisturbed snow. "Russ, do you—" She turned to face him, but two empty chairs sat on the other side of the table. "Where'd they go?"

Together she and Carter scanned the empty kitchen.

"This is awkward," he said.

"This whole day is awkward. But I'd say this is par for the course."

Carter perked up like a dog spotting a tennis ball. "Do you golf too?"

"Yeah. My brother taught me."

"What's your brother do?"

Not ready to share that tidbit, she stood, scraping the chair legs across the tile floor. "Let's save that for another time. As long as you're here, should we find Russ and Ashley and make lunch?"

"Are you inviting me to lunch at someone else's house?"

"Listen, we can fight this or go with it. If we fight it, Kathleen will just try again. If we go with it, we can enjoy a good meal and maybe some good company—if you don't get all nerdy on me again."

"You're the one talking about farm waste and renewable energy."

She laughed. "Would you rather talk about dead people?"

"Of course." He walked around the table and smiled down at her, his blue eyes bright. "But I'd talk about almost anything with you."

Jess wanted to groan, but Carter's smile and those eyes—if she wasn't already committed to fixing her reputation, she might run away again to avoid the temptation.

Chapter Eight

J ess sat at the kitchen table swirling her French fries in barbecue sauce as she reviewed Russell Farms' marketing budget and past campaigns. She could see Russ and Tom's influence all over the ads—Russ's insistence on mentioning their all-natural techniques and products with several photos she recognized from Tom's portfolio. They weren't bad ad campaigns, but there was always room for improvement.

The back door swooshed open. The familiar thud of her dad's work boots hit the mudroom floor. "How's it going, Smooch?"

"Good. I finally organized the office, so I can work on the fun stuff now." As he walked into the kitchen, she slid two ads across the table toward him. "Do you remember seeing these ads?"

"You know I don't pay attention to that sort of thing," he said, but he looked at the flyers anyway. "I'm sure I did, but I already know where I'm going to buy my produce. I don't need an ad."

That's what she suspected. They needed to target tourists, not locals. "Thanks for the feedback. How's the car?"

"Tuned up and ready to go." He sat at the retro chrome diner-style table and stole some fries.

"You don't have to work on my car in your free time. I can go to a mechanic, and you could get a hobby."

"Cars are my hobby. Don't try to take that away from me." He winked at her.

She pushed the rest of her fries over to him. "I don't think a hobby is supposed to be work, but I won't argue." Her phone tweeted, so she checked the text message.

Thx for your help! Six for six on calls today. Everyone wants to help.

She smiled. Carter would have figured it out on his own, but she liked knowing she'd helped. *My pleasure. Did Kathleen ever call back?*

Better question: will she stop calling?

That time she laughed. Jess could only imagine how excited Russ's mom was to have someone young interested in the museum. Her one complaint in life was that the youngest museum volunteer was sixty years old.

I asked about the setup.

Jess gasped. *Why??* Everyone in town knew about Kathleen's interfering, but no one ever called her on it. It wasn't polite to meddle with a meddler. Three dots blinked on her phone screen as she waited for Carter's reply.

Why wouldn't I?

What kind of question was that? He clearly didn't understand the ways of small-town grandmothers. Or Kathleen. *Because that's just what she does.*

How was I supposed to know that?

IDK. Ask ME next time.

Felix shuffled into the kitchen and went straight to the refrigerator. "Who's the guy?"

Jess looked around the cramped kitchen with its 1990s oak cabinets and linoleum floors to make sure she hadn't missed something. Her dad ate the last fry, but as far as she could tell they were the only ones there. "What guy?"

"The one you're texting."

She pressed the phone to her chest. "How do you know I'm texting a guy?"

"Humming."

"Who's humming?"

"You were. You hum anytime you're dating someone." He pulled out a soda before turning to smile at her. "So, who is it?"

She wanted to be creeped out or offended that her brother knew that about her when she hadn't even recognized it herself, but both emotions crumpled beneath the fear that filled every cell in her body. Pale and sweaty, her brother looked at her with glassy eyes. "Felix," she whispered before she could stop herself.

He tensed. "I'm not using. I'm just not feeling well."

She wanted to believe him—every ounce of her wanted to—but she'd heard and seen it all before. Still, she wouldn't call him on his lie until she had proof, so she forced a smile and said, "Okay."

Her dad patted her hand as he stood. "The news in on."

Jess's phone tweeted as he walked into the living room, but she ignored it. She couldn't text while a hundred different memories bombarded her—trips to the hospital, stolen money, and fights about if and when to kick Felix out of the house. She couldn't prove it, but she was pretty sure that's what had pushed her mom over the edge and out of the house. How would she and Dad handle it if Felix relapsed?

The chair groaned as Felix plopped himself onto it. "I knew you wouldn't believe me, not that I blame you. I wouldn't believe me either."

The sadness on his face stabbed at her heart. "I believe you," she lied.

He snorted. "No, you don't, but thanks for trying to make me feel better. I know it doesn't prove anything, but I'm going to a meeting tonight, if that makes you feel better."

"A little." If he actually went. "Why don't I drive you?"

"Sure."

"Really? That was easier than I expected."

"Because I'm not using, so I'm not trying to avoid meetings. I actually wouldn't mind a ride. I didn't sleep well last night."

Jess checked the time. "When do you want to leave?"

He looked over his shoulder at the clock behind him. "There's an AA meeting at St. Luke's at eight."

More than an hour away. "There's an NA meeting in Charlevoix at seven."

"You want to drive all the way into Charlevoix?"

Her chest ached. "I want to make sure my brother gets help as quickly as possible. If that means driving to Charlevoix, I'll drive to Charlevoix."

He squeezed her arm with his clammy hand. "Thank you."

She nodded. Not sure what to say, she asked, "Are you going to wear that?"

He looked down at his John Deere t-shirt. "What's wrong with it?"

"Just because you're an addict doesn't mean you have to look like one. Go change."

"Fine, but then we should leave."

"I'll wait for you in the car."

As Felix went upstairs to change, Jess went outside to cry.

#

"I'll be done in an hour." Felix climbed out of Jess's car. "Do you want to go into town? I can call you when I'm done."

"I might. If I'm not here, call me."

He gave her a weak smile. "Thanks again."

She nodded, not trusting her voice. She'd managed to stop the tears long enough to get to town without her brother noticing, but she didn't trust herself not to cry in the coffee shop. The last thing she wanted to do—besides watch her brother relapse—was cry about it in public. Instead of risking it, she tilted back the driver's seat and closed her eyes. She was tired enough to fall asleep. She just hoped she didn't drool.

Her phone tweeted.

Carter!

She'd completely forgotten about their conversation. Picking up the phone, she went straight to text messages.

Next time? Do you think someone will try to set us up again? Sent almost forty-five minutes ago.

Everything okay? Sent a moment ago.

How did she answer that question?

Before she could, her phone dinged again. *Are you in Charlevoix?*

Jess sat up as she stared at her phone's screen. That was creepy. Why would he—

A horn beeped.

She spun in her seat, dropping her phone as she looked for the culprit. Parked beside her sat Carter. He smiled and waved. Her jaw dropped open as she tried to figure out what he was doing there.

While she stared at him, he climbed out of his car, walked toward her, and opened her door. His clean scent drifted toward her when he bent over and made eye contact. "It is you."

"Um, hi."

"Hi. Am I interrupting anything?"

She glanced at the community building. Did he know what happened there at seven o'clock on Wednesday nights? "No, I'm waiting for my brother. What are you doing here?"

"I live here."

"I thought you lived in Petoskey."

"I work in Petoskey. I live just outside of Charlevoix. What are you doing while you wait? Do you want some company?"

"In my car?"

He laughed. "Or we could walk down to the marina. It's a nice night."

"Sure, yeah. That makes more sense." She climbed out of her car. Carter stepped back to give her room. The breeze was indeed warm for April, but it still sent a chill through her, so she grabbed Felix's sweatshirt from the back seat and slipped into it. It hung down to mid-thigh, but it would keep her warm. Locking the car, she smiled at Carter. "Lead the way."

He grabbed a jacket from his car before heading past her toward the community center. Jess's heart clenched as they walked past the people who were hopefully helping her brother. As soon as they cleared the edge of the building, her whole body relaxed. As they walked in silence, she took in their route. The flower-lined sidewalk took them around the community center's lawn and down a short decline before angling them toward the marina.

"I never knew this path was here," she said.

"Do you spend a lot of time at the community center?"

"No, why?"

"Then there's no reason for you to know it's here."

"Do *you* spend a lot of time at the community center?"

"No, but I spent two weeks walking the town when I moved here."

"Why?"

He shrugged. "Why not? I was going to live here so I wanted to know my way around. I found all kinds of secluded paths. This one's pretty busy during the Venetian Festival, though. People park at the center, then walk to the marina for fireworks."

A few steps later, sailboat masts peeked over the horizon. Then boats. The slap of water against hulls mixed with the twittering birds. Jess's footsteps clapped against the cement as Carter led her to a bench. As they sat, he zipped up his plain navy coat. The crisp, smooth material creased as he moved. She'd never seen anything like it.

"Is there a stain?" he asked, following her gaze.

"Sorry, no. I was just thinking I've never seen a coat like that before."

His eyebrows rose. "It's just a coat."

"I know. That's why it's so weird. It's not a hoodie or a Carhartt. I think you're the only man I know under fifty who doesn't wear one."

"That's weird."

"*You're* weird."

He pointed to the Lake Superior State University logo on her sweatshirt. "I thought you went to Michigan State University."

She wrapped her arms around her middle, hugging the soft material to her stomach. "This is my brother's."

"He graduated from Lake Superior State."

"He went there, but he didn't graduate."

"What's he do now?"

Jess tried to figure out what to say. It had been so long since she'd met anyone who didn't know her family's history that she didn't want to ruin the illusion, but she also liked Carter. It had been a while since she'd been able to talk and tease so comfortably with someone. He hadn't avoided her yet. Might as well tell him everything.

Taking a deep breath, she turned in her seat to face him. "At this very moment, my brother's at a Narcotics Anonymous meeting. During the day, and when he's sober, he's an electrician."

Carter blew out a long breath. "I'm sorry."

Her pride prepared for battle. "For what?"

"For how hard that must be for all of you. How's he doing now?"

"He's been clean for a year, but I think he might be using again."

"I don't know what I can do to help, but if you need anything, let me know."

Jess studied him as suspicion gnawed at her. "That's it? Don't you want to know what happened? Aren't you going to blame me or my parents for letting this happen?"

His eyes widened. "Who did that?"

"A lot of people."

"Well, they're idiots."

She didn't know what to say to that. Even her best friends had insinuated that she could or should have done something to help Felix.

He nudged her with his elbow. "I've done a lot of genealogy research. I've spoken to several people who had addicts in their families. It's never someone else's fault."

An unexpected comfort warmed her insides. "Thanks for that. This is usually when I defend myself and my family." She offered Carter a smile, hoping it expressed her sincerity.

"Do you want to talk about why you think your brother's using?"

Jess slouched against the back of the bench, folding her arm beneath her head. "His hands are clammy and his eyes are glassy. He said he's sick, but he's said that before."

"How long ago did he start using?"

"Eight years." She rubbed her hand across the well-worn sweatshirt logo. "Felix played hockey at LSSU. His junior year, someone cross-checked him in a game—I'll spare you the gory details—and he ended up having six back surgeries. By the time he started his last round of physical therapy, he was hooked. He barely made it through the first semester his senior year, but he was too high to bother going back for the second half."

Carter swiveled so he was facing her. "What'd he do?"

"We don't know. He disappeared for almost a year, then came back when he ran out of money. He spent the next seven years lying, stealing, and in and out of rehab."

"I can't imagine the toll that took on your family."

"My dad and I did the best we could. My mom couldn't handle it, so she ran off with her best friend's husband."

"Oh, God. I'm so sorry."

"It wasn't all bad. When my mom left, something in Felix flipped. He went to rehab and stayed. He's been clean ever since." She sighed. "Until today."

"Do you think something happened?"

"I don't know. I left town after I had my meltdown, so I was gone when he got clean. He and my dad aren't the chattiest people, so I don't know everything that happened while I was gone."

"I wish I had some inspirational words of wisdom for you, but I don't really know what to say."

His honesty relieved her. "I appreciate that. People always want to make me feel better, but they quote motivational memes instead just listening."

"I'm a good listener. Comes with the job."

"Teaching?"

"Genealogy. I take in a lot of oral history. I have to be a good listener."

"That makes sense." The morose horn of the local ferry filled the air, but it didn't darken Jess's mood. "I'm grateful. It's never been so easy to talk about my brother before."

"I'm sorry about that."

She elbowed him. "No more apologies. You've convinced me you're an amazing guy. I get it."

"That wasn't my intention." But he smiled. "Just trying to show you that good guys aren't always wrapped in Carhartts."

She laughed, surprised at how much she enjoyed his company. Carter's presence—at the farm and at the marina—more than compensated for the weirdness of working for Russ. Now she needed to figure out a way to keep him working there. "How are things going with your program?"

"Those leads you gave me were great. I have four meetings scheduled for next week."

"You'll have your list of partners in no time."

"I hope so. Having so many local, small historical organizations could be helpful or frustrating. I haven't figured out which yet."

"How so?"

He raised his left hand. "On the one hand, they've already collected a ton of information. It'll be easier for the students to get their feet wet and get started in ancestry." Lowering his left hand, he raised his right. "On the other hand, there are always a few volunteers in each organization who have an agenda. They aren't as interested in helping others as they are in telling people whatever information is important to them. They're usually the sweetest old men and women, though, so it's hard to cut them off."

"But won't that be a good experience for the students too? It'll teach them how to be good listeners."

He shrugged. "Maybe. So many of my students can carry on whole conversations via text, yet they can't articulate themselves verbally when they have questions or want to share an observation."

Jess had to chuckle. "I've met a few people like that. When I started at the bank, part of my training included a half-day session on cell phone etiquette and the dos and don'ts of professional conversations."

"I might need to look into that. I don't hold anything against my students and their communication techniques, but they need to learn how to talk with the older generations too. It's definitely a learned skill."

Church bells chimed, and Jess checked her watch. "Thirty more minutes." She turned away from Carter to take in the view. "We should probably take advantage of the marina while we're here."

"What will you say to your brother after the meeting?"

"We'll probably stop for hamburgers, then go home." And search for drugs.

A seagull squawked overhead as traffic whooshed behind them. The scents of diesel and fish wafted on the breeze, reminding Jess to check Felix's tackle box.

"Has your brother's behavior changed recently?"

"What?" She pulled her focus from the catamaran in front of her and turned to Carter.

He stared out over the water. "Even if you don't know your brother as well as you used to, you're familiar with his routine. If it hasn't changed, why not give him the benefit of the doubt? People get sick sometimes."

"I know."

"It's okay to be cautiously optimistic, isn't it?"

She used to think so. "Even a little optimism can be heartbreaking."

He squeezed her shoulder. "Whatever you decide to do, I'll be here if you need to talk."

Jess hoped she wouldn't have to call him, but if she did ... she smiled.

Chapter Nine

J ess knocked on Gran's door. Three seconds later, it opened, and
  Gran pushed Jess further into the hallway. "Let's go, sweetheart. I
want to get out of here."

Jess let herself be pushed toward the care home's entrance. "Hello
to you too. I'm fine, thanks. Work's good."

"Don't be dramatic. You went to work. You went home. You probably did laundry. Am I right?"

"I helped Dad repaint the front porch."

Gran snorted as they stepped through the front door of the nursing
home and into the midmorning sun. Not quite above them, the sun
took the chill out of the air, but it wasn't warm yet. That didn't bother
Gran, though. Her navy floral sweatshirt apparently kept her warm
enough as she marched down the sidewalk and across the parking lot,
right to Jess's car.

"How do you know where I'm parked?"

Gran pointed a thumb over her shoulder without turning around.
"I have a window."

Jess unlocked the car so Gran could get in. By the time Jess climbed in, Gran was already buckled up. "Where are we going?"

"Pearl serves leftover prime rib and eggs on Saturday mornings. I'm famished."

"Famished?"

"I wouldn't expect you to understand. You've never had the same breakfast seven days a week."

Jess slid the car into drive and headed into town. "I thought you had options."

"We do, but the only thing tolerable is the oatmeal. I'm too old to eat oatmeal every day. Do you have any idea what that does to my bowels?"

If she hadn't been driving, Jess would have closed her eyes and said a silent prayer. Instead, she pressed on the accelerator. "Let's get you some prime rib and eggs."

"And coffee. I miss coffee."

"They have coffee at the farm."

"Sure, if you like coffee-scented brown water."

"Now you're just being picky. They serve the same coffee at Pearl's." Gran huffed.

Jess rolled her eyes. "Why are you so cranky today?"

"Sorry, it must be rubbing off on me."

"From where?"

"One of my neighbors is the whiniest woman I've ever met. Every time I point out the good things in life, she has something else to complain about."

"Maybe you should spend time with one of your other neighbors."

"I would, but she makes the best gingersnaps you've ever tasted." Gran opened her purse and pulled out a clear bag of cookies. "I think I understand Felix better now that I've had Marilyn's cookies. I think I'd do about anything for a bag of these. Al loves them too. You remember Al, don't you?"

Jess held in a groan. "I don't believe I've met him."

"He's the computer whiz. Born and raised in northern Michigan. He'll be at the farm again this afternoon. I can introduce you."

Jess hoped to be home and in the middle of a good book by the afternoon, but she didn't want to upset Gran. Instead, she ate a cookie—truly the best gingersnap she'd ever tasted—on their way to their favorite Boyne Heights café. Gran only lived a few miles away from Pearl's, but by the time they found a parking spot and made it inside, the tables were full.

"Do you want to wait or go somewhere else?" Jess asked.

"Let's sit over there." Gran pointed to the far side of the room where Ashley waved at them. Russ turned in his seat and lifted a hand when he saw them.

Before Jess could protest, Gran was halfway across the restaurant. She'd already taken a seat next to Russ and across from Ashley by the time Jess made it to the square, four-person table. "We don't mean to intrude," she said, looking at Ashley, then glaring at her grandmother.

"Of course we do," Gran said. "If we don't, we won't get a table."

"We wouldn't have waved if we wanted you to stay away." Ashley nudged out Jess's chair. "We just ordered, but I'm sure we can get Pearl to add yours to the ticket. Do you need a menu?"

Gran waved her off. "Pearl's been serving the same grub for twenty years."

"Because it's good grub," Pearl said, stepping up to their table. "Dorothy, are you harassing my customers?"

"I'm one of your customers." Gran tapped the pad in Pearl's apron pocket. "Why don't you take our orders?"

As Jess took a seat, she noticed Ashley's wide eyes. "They're putting on a show," she whispered. "My grandma and Pearl go to the same church and have been friends for longer than I've been alive."

Ashley smiled. "I hope I make friends like that someday."

So did Jess, for Ashley and for herself.

Pearl nudged Jess with her hip. "What're you having, sweetheart?"

"I'll have whatever Gran ordered."

"I'll send someone over with your coffee."

"Decaf for you?" Gran asked, looking at Ashley.

"Wh ... why would you ask?" Russ's wife blushed all the way up to her hairline.

"I was an OB/GYN nurse for thirty years. I can tell."

"We haven't told my mom yet," Russ said, pulling Ashley's chair around the corner and closer to him. "Can you keep it a secret until tomorrow? She's coming over tonight for dinner. I'm sure the whole county will know by tomorrow night."

"I'll have to be careful this afternoon, but I'm sure I can do it."

"This afternoon?" Jess looked at Gran. "What are you doing this afternoon?"

"We're going to the museum after breakfast. Didn't I mention it?"

"It must have slipped your mind."

"What are you doing at the museum?" Ashley asked.

"Kathleen called me this week to see if I could help her identify some photos and other artifacts. I already had plans with Jess, so I figured we could go over together. I can't drive myself, you see."

"Did you bring your magnifying glass?" Jess asked, trying to imagine her visually impaired grandmother identifying anything.

"Kathleen has one for me."

Of course she did. Jess checked her watch. "How long will it take you to sort through everything?"

Gran shrugged. "She has a few boxes of things, and she has a young man with her who might have some questions."

Jess tensed as their server filled everyone's coffee cups. When she looked at Russ, he was clenching his jaw. Ashley bit her lips together but her shoulders shook. Once the waitress was gone, Jess gave Gran her full attention. "Carter's going to be there?"

"That's his name." Her grandma smiled. "Do you know him? Kathleen seemed particularly smitten."

"I'm sure she is. And I suppose it was her idea that you bring me?"

"She knows you drive me everywhere."

"I'm sorry," Russ said. "I'll talk to her about it tonight."

"You'll have more important things to talk about. Don't worry about it." Jess tried to offer a reassuring smile, but her stomach flipped.

Ashley asked Gran a dozen questions about the museum while they waited, giving Jess plenty of time to run through possible afternoon scenarios. None of them ended well. She needed to figure out what to do about Carter. Then Kathleen. Before she'd formulated a solid plan, Pearl returned with their meals.

"Jessica, are you still a magician with flowers?" she asked as she set a plate full of steaming food in front of Jess.

"I can't pull a bouquet out of my purse if that's what you mean." Her stomach rumbled as the scents of butter, bacon, and cinnamon filled her head.

"Don't be silly. It's my planters out front. The last three years I've planted flowers and they've all died. If I can't get something to grow this year, I'm giving up."

"I can probably help with that. What have you tried?"

Pearl tucked the tray under her arm as she counted off on her fingers. "Begonias, impatiens, and marigolds. I've grown all of those in the past, but now everything dies."

Jess pictured the brick front of the restaurant with its white trim and yellow door. But hadn't there been an awning over the window? She turned in her seat so she could see. "Do you still have that green awning out front?"

"Heavens, no. The ice ripped it down a few winters ago and I didn't replace it. The horrid thing never matched anyway."

"It didn't." Jess turned her focus back to Pearl. "But it provided some shade for your plants. You need to either replace the awning or get some flowers that like full sunshine."

The older woman beamed. "I knew I could count on you. I almost joined the garden club to see if they could help, but I wanted to ask you first. Will you be giving any more talks at the club this year?"

"Not this year."

Pearl *tsk*ed. "That's probably because they don't know you're back yet. I'll tell them I saw you here. See if they don't call you in a week or two." She winked before dashing away.

Before Jess even started eating, Ashley had eaten half her food, but between bites she asked, "You're a member of the garden club?"

It was Jess's turn to blush. "No, but I love flowers and have a knack for growing them. It's always been a hobby. I used to speak to the garden club once or twice a year to talk about new flower varieties and growing techniques that I'd studied."

Ashley shook her head, then took another bite of her pancakes. "I can't even grow weeds. I noticed some empty flower beds around the house. Maybe you could recommend something for us."

Before she answered, Jess glanced at Russ. He shrugged. "Go for it. Just make sure it's something a pregnant lady can take care of."

Ashley smacked his arm, but Jess smiled. It had been a few years since she'd played with flowers. She wouldn't mind getting her hands dirty again. *After* she talked with Kathleen.

#

Jess jiggled the knob of the museum's front door. Locked. She knocked, then turned to where her grandma stood at the bottom of the front steps. "Why's it locked?"

"The museum's closed until Memorial Day. Let's try the back door." She disappeared around the corner.

The heels of Jess's ankle boots clicked on the cement as she descended the steps of the converted church. Sunlight glowed off the pale yellow paint. When she passed the long, narrow stained glass windows, she tried to imagine what the light looked like shining through them. She hadn't been to church since she'd moved back to Boyne. Something about the historic building made her want to go again.

Instead, she followed her meddling grandma into a church where Gran's matchmaking friend waited. What could possibly go wrong?

Gran let herself in through the back door. Jess followed her into a room stacked high with boxes. They followed a path through the boxes, past the bathrooms, and up thickly carpeted stairs. The higher they climbed, the clearer the voices became. Jess could pick Kathleen's laugh out of a crowd of meddling mothers. Mixed with it was a warm, deep tone that had to be Carter.

He really wasn't like any guy Jess had ever met. He was probably as sweet and patient with Kathleen as he'd been with Jess that night in Charlevoix. At least he'd make her afternoon at the museum enjoyable, even if she didn't particularly care to learn the history of each of her neighbors.

When they reached the upper level, they stepped into the former sanctuary. Oak pews still filled the center of the space, but shelves and banquet tables lined the walls. As she walked toward Kathleen, Jess admired the nearest table full of glass and wooden toys. Toddler-sized lace-trimmed dresses hung on the walls behind antique wooden cribs.

"Jess." The surprise in Carter's voice grabbed her attention. "What are you doing here?" He met her halfway up the aisle.

She pointed over her shoulder with her thumb. "My grandma's a friend of Kathleen. Apparently she volunteered to help organize pictures today. I'm her ride."

"You don't have to stay if you don't want to. I can take your grandma home when we're done."

Jess shrugged. "Honestly, I don't have anything else to do. If I go home, I'll probably have to help my dad paint the shed."

"Not exactly enthusiasm, but I'll take it." He led her to a workspace where he sat down behind a laptop computer. Kathleen made introductions before escorting Gran to a box of documents on the other side of the large table. As Jess sat beside Carter, he asked, "Can I get you anything?"

"Like what?"

"I don't know. It seemed like I should offer something."

Jess pulled her phone out of her purse. "We just stuffed ourselves at Pearl's, so I'll be good for a while. Don't let me bother you. I'll check my email."

"You're welcome to help sort," Kathleen said, pushing a pile of letters toward her. "Elaine Court donated these. She didn't look at everything in the boxes, so we need to figure out what we have, then we can decide what to do with it."

Jess counted twenty envelopes in the stack. If it took five minutes to read each letter, it would take almost two hours to finish. She was sure Gran would want to stay longer than that. Reading the letters would help kill some of the time, though. Then she could check email. With as much excitement as she could muster, she picked up the top envelope and pulled out the letter.

Dear William,

The weather continues to plague us. We haven't had rain for weeks, and the corn is suffering. Our neighbor, Mr. Crawford, has agreed to help me try a new irrigation technique—

"This is a farm report," she said, checking the date in the upper right corner. Nineteen ten. Interesting. She'd never given much thought to the area's earlier farming techniques. What did Joe and Mr. Crawford do? Did it work?

She kept reading about Joe Johnson and his wife, Elizabeth; Mr. Levi Crawford and his wife and four children; and the letter's recipient, William, Joe's brother. Living in different parts of Michigan, they'd relied on these letters to discuss their farms, families, and faith. They not only experimented with irrigation techniques, they discussed new planting and harvesting styles and even debated the quality of cow manure versus pig manure as fertilizers for their crops and gardens. Jess's fingers itched for a keyboard to take notes.

Carter nudged her foot with his. "You're pretty quiet. What's so interesting?"

"These farm reports between brothers." She held up a letter. "It's fascinating. If we knew where their farms were, we could track the history of the land usage as well as how successful their techniques were. I wonder if the National Weather Service has a history of weather patterns that far back. These letters could help verify their reports or fill in any holes. That could show us if there've been any weather patterns over the past century and how they impacted these farming techniques."

He tapped her foot again. When she looked at him, he winked. "Look at that. Interesting dead people for the farm nerd."

Jess rolled her eyes. "If you had told me how cool this information was, I might have agreed to help you sooner."

"Between brothers?" Kathleen asked, reaching for the letters. "Which ones?"

"Joe and William Johnson. Do you have any more you want me to read through?"

"Would you?"

Jess accepted another stack of envelopes and had to admit that she couldn't wait to find out what was inside.

Before she started reading, Kathleen asked, "Dorothy, do you have plans for the last weekend of the month?"

"Not unless Jessica has something up her sleeve." Kathleen and Gran both looked at Jess. "Do you?"

"It's three weeks away. I haven't thought about it yet."

Kathleen smiled. "Then you should join us at the farmhouse. All the kids and their families will be there, plus a few of our longtime employees and their families. You're one of us now. You need to be there."

"What's the occasion?" Gran asked.

"We can't celebrate Memorial Day as a family because that's opening weekend of the market and there's always something happening in town or at the museum, so a few years before my husband died, we started having picnics the last weekend in April. Sometimes it rains, sometimes it snows, but we always have fun."

Gran clapped once and smiled. "How exciting! I'll make sure Felix and my son are there."

"I, uh ..." Jess wasn't really sure how to respond. She'd always wanted to be part of the Russell family—maybe more than she'd actually wanted to be with Russ—but she didn't want a pity invite. Then again, it was the first invite she'd gotten since she'd moved back to town, and she was an employee, so it made sense to invite her.

"Carter, you should come too. I want to introduce you to the rest of my kids—prove to them there are some smart, young adults out there who see the value in preserving our past."

Jess forced herself not to roll her eyes.

"I'd be honored." He gave a disarming smile. Gran and Kathleen went back to work while Jess overthought the invitation. Then Carter leaned toward her. "You have to come now. I won't know anyone else."

"You know Gran and Kathleen."

"I won't know anyone my age."

This time she did roll her eyes. "You know Russ and Ashley."

"They'll be busy."

She leaned toward him and whispered, "Why are you afraid to go alone?"

"What if Kathleen tries to set me up again?"

Jess hadn't considered another setup. She glanced across the table. Gran and Kathleen twittered away, apparently unaware of their companions. "You make a good point. New plan. We run interference for each other. Deal?"

"Deal." He smiled.

Butterflies swarmed her stomach.

Only one problem remained. Who would run interference between Carter and Jess?

Chapter Ten

J ess pulled up in front of the salon. "I'll pick you up in an hour."

"Better make it two." Gran climbed out of the car. "I don't want to have to rush."

Jess waited until Gran stepped into the salon before pulling back onto the road and heading south through Petoskey. Five minutes later she parked at CNMC and headed for the Kresge building. Would Carter think it weird that she'd looked up his office hours online? Well, if he didn't want people to know when to find him there, he shouldn't put them on the college's website.

She passed several classrooms before approaching a cluster of offices midway down the hall. Three doors were closed, but three were open, including Carter's. He sat at his desk in front of a wide window, grading papers. Jess still had time to slip away before he saw her, but instead she knocked. "Are you busy?"

He looked up and froze. "What are you doing here?"

"Gran's stylist moved to Petoskey earlier this year. I drive her up every week to get cut and styled. You don't mind that I'm here, do you?" She pointed around the sparse and tidy office. Two guest chairs sat in front of the desk with a low credenza behind it, flush against the wall below the window. Two organized bookcases flanked the desk on either wall. Besides the black office phone, the only other thing on the desk was the stack of papers. "You're busy. I should leave."

"No, don't." He stood and smiled, motioning to the chairs. "You caught me by surprise, that's all. Have a seat. I welcome the interruption."

"Good, because I forgot to bring a book with me." She sat in the surprisingly comfortable chair. "Any good papers in there?"

He sat and leaned back, tossing his pen onto the desk. "It's anyone's guess. I have some students with great content but horrible writing skills. Some with great writing skills but hardly any research. A couple of standouts and a couple I may be seeing again next semester."

"What's the topic?"

"Michigan history."

"Which part?"

"Any part. It's the final paper. I like to give them as many options as possible. Some of the students prefer the fur-trading era and others go with Henry or Gerald Ford. This semester I have one on Motown, though. That's a first. I'm looking forward to reading that one."

"That's quite the final topic."

"Wait a sec." His grin widened as he grabbed the papers and shuffled through them. He stopped and handed her a paper. "You'll appreciate this."

She took it and laughed. "The History of Cherries in Emmet County, 1875 to 1900. Clearly this kid's a smart one."

"I thought you'd approve. So, what're you doing while Gran's getting pretty?"

Jess shrugged. "That's why I'm here. The website says your office hours end in thirty minutes. Do you have any plans for lunch?"

He raised an eyebrow. "Are you asking me out?"

She cringed. "No." Or was she?

"Good. I thought we weren't doing that, so I was confused."

"Don't be. I just figured you'd need to eat lunch too, so why not eat together?"

"I'd love to." He picked up his pen. "Give me thirty minutes."

She stood. "I'll wait outside. Text me when you're done."

"You're going to sit in your car?"

"Why not? It's a nice day."

Carter pointed at a bookcase. "Find something to read. I'll finish grading papers."

"Don't you have students coming in?"

"No one made an appointment. If anyone shows up and needs privacy, I'll let you know." He didn't wait for her to respond before returning to the assignments.

Not wanting to interrupt, Jess took his suggestion and investigated his book collection. Michigan history. American history. Native American history. Biographies. *Nevada Rose*? She pulled out that book and read the back cover.

Eliza Montgomery, a pregnant widow, is forced to marry rancher Dutch Sawyer while standing on her first husband's fresh grave. Dutch isn't thrilled about the match to a spoiled, rich woman, but it's either that or let her ruthless neighbor marry her for her land. Can Dutch and Eliza turn their convenient situation into a real marriage?

"Oh my gosh." Jess spun around, laughing. "You read historical romance novels!"

Carter looked up, his face twisted. "So?"

"I've never met a guy who openly reads romance novels." She took the book back to the

chair and plopped into the seat. "Is it any good?"

"I wouldn't keep it if it wasn't."

Her eyes widened. "You've actually read it?"

"Of course I've read it. Why would I keep a book I've never read?"

"I don't know. Maybe someone gave it to you as a joke."

He cocked his head to the side. "Or maybe I'm comfortable enough with who I am to admit that I enjoy a good historical novel, even if the plot revolves around a love story."

Jess couldn't help smiling at the intelligent, attractive, sappy-hearted man on the other side of the table. "You're *such* a nerd."

He rolled his eyes and went back to work. Jess shrugged and opened the book. Eliza watched from behind a bush as Dutch filled in her husband's grave. She tried not to cry, but her husband had left her pregnant and alone on a farm she couldn't run in a place she didn't understand with people she didn't know. Desperate to squelch her grief, she started to run toward the grave to throw herself in, but her dress caught on the bush's branches and she fell. Lester Straight yanked her off the ground and up behind the hard saddle horn. She struggled. Dutch came to her rescue. The parson told everyone what had to happen—Eliza needed a husband to provide for and protect her. Who would it be?

"Are you about done?"

Jess dropped the book.

Carter chuckled. "It's good, isn't it?"

Fumbling for calm, she straightened herself and the book. "You have great taste in romance novels."

"I know. You can take that with you if you want."

"No way." She put it back on the shelf, laying it horizontally in front of the rest of the books. "If I take it with me, I won't have anything to read next week."

Carter pointed at the shelf before stuffing his papers into a messenger bag. "I have six books by that author, plus a bunch more."

"If I like how this one ends, I'll consider taking another one home. Where do you want to go to lunch?"

"Shouldn't we wait for Gran?" Carter walked around the desk toward the door.

Jess followed him out of the office and down the hall. "No, she usually eats at the salon."

"What kind of salon is it?" The twisted expression on his face made Jess laugh.

"It turns into a potluck when Gran's there. She brought a pan of brownies. I don't know what everyone else brings, but she's always full when we go home."

"There's a Mediterranean place past the river I've been wanting to try. Sound good?"

"Perfect."

As soon as they stepped outside, someone said, "Jess Miller?"

She and Carter turned simultaneously toward the slender, casually dressed woman approaching them. Average height, average size, with a blond pixie cut and wearing jeans, a khaki jacket, and aviator glasses. It took several seconds for the unextraordinary but not unattractive appearance to register. "Sharon?"

Her high school teammate smiled as she took off her glasses. "What a pleasant surprise. How are you, Carter?"

"Just on my way to lunch. You two know each other?"

"We played softball together in high school." Sharon elbowed Jess. "I was a senior when Jess was a freshman, but we had one good season together."

"She's exaggerating. I was a glorified bat girl that year."

"But still on varsity."

As if that mattered anymore. "Are you still coaching softball at Petoskey High School?" Jess asked.

"I'm here now." Sharon opened her arms. "This is my second season as head coach for CNMC. I also assist the athletic director in the off-season. What brings you to campus?"

Jess nodded toward Carter. "Lunch."

"And how do *you* two know each other?" Sharon asked.

"We met at work ... sort of," she said. "I was at work, anyway."

"I've been consulting with Russell Farms in Boyne Heights to try to create a genealogy work-study program in the area."

Sharon's eyes widened and she grabbed Jess's arm. "You work at Russell Farms?"

"I do." And despite how much she loved it, Sharon's reaction and tone managed to drain the enjoyment out of it. "I just started. Carter and I actually met on my first day."

"Is it temporary? You're not working there full-time, are you?"

"I am."

"Oh." Sharon released Jess and smiled, but it didn't take a psychologist to recognize the awkwardness of the gesture. "I hope it works out for you. If it doesn't, though, you really should take some classes here. I have several players who've loved Carter's classes. Maybe you'll find something else you love and switch careers."

The idea wasn't inherently offensive, but somehow Sharon's suggestion made Jess feel like she should consider a career change or a retirement home. She plastered on her own fake smile. "I'll think about it. We should get going, though. We need to hurry back so I don't keep Carter from his afternoon office hours."

"I don't—"

Jess pushed him toward the parking lot before he could finish explaining that he didn't have afternoon office hours. "It was good seeing you again, Sharon. Good luck this season."

Sharon probably gave a polite farewell, but Jess tuned it out. She didn't need to hear it. Running into Sharon had confirmed her fears—small towns didn't forget. Jess had her work cut out for her.

Chapter Eleven

For the next two weeks, Jess dropped Gran off at the salon, then let herself into Carter's office to read until he was ready for lunch. They were only interrupted once by a student, when Jess quietly took her book outside and read in the hallway until the coast was clear. She never saw Sharon again. Maybe Sharon was really the ghost of seasons past sent to remind Jess how much she still had to atone for. If only Carter hadn't seen her too.

When Jess wasn't playing chauffeur or working, she stopped by the nursery to check on the flower inventory. The owner, a friend of her father's, helped her flag photos in a book to show Pearl what her options would look like once they bloomed. Together, Jess and Pearl picked three full-sun varieties for each planter to make sure the restaurant had flowers blooming in spring, summer, and fall. She also called the garden and 4-H clubs, as well as the county fairground, volunteering wherever she could. She didn't particularly care to work in the rabbit and chicken barn, but she smiled while she was there so everyone could see how calm and professional she was.

Except she wasn't. Some of the volunteer hours spilled into her work hours, which was why she popped in at work on the morning of the Russells' pre-Memorial Day party. The day before, her chat with the executive director of the fair had taken longer than expected, but it would be worth it if she could arrange the Russell Farms sponsorship for one of the events.

Jess had almost caught up on her emails when her dad called. "Hey," she answered with a smile. "Did you see my note? I didn't mean to sneak out, but I wanted to finish some work so I can enjoy the picnic this afternoon. You're still coming with me, right?"

"I'll try, but I don't know if I'll make it. I'm taking Felix to the hospital."

The tremor started in Jess's hand. She closed her eyes and took a deep breath, willing her heart rate to slow down. "What's wrong?"

"He fell down the stairs."

"Was he drunk?"

"No."

"What's he on?" Someone mumbled in the background. Tears filled her eyes. "What's his excuse this time?"

"He swears he's clean, Smooch. Something's wrong. His temp's over a hundred. He got dizzy and missed a step."

That was a new excuse. Jess wanted to side with her dad—she wanted to believe her brother—but too many years of emergency room visits had taken their toll. "If you don't make it, I'll make a plate for you and bring it home."

"I'll call you after we talk to the doctor."

"Not this time, Dad." Her voice cracked. "I want to enjoy the party. I'll see you later and you can tell me about it then."

She disconnected the call before he made another excuse. Or worse, before Felix could take the phone and plead with her again. She'd already missed so many events and activities over the years because of him. She wanted to enjoy one last event before word spread about "that Miller family."

The office door opened, startling her. Wiping off her cheeks, she turned to greet the visitor.

"What's wrong?" Jess recognized Ashley's voice before her eyes had cleared enough to focus on her face. Her ex's wife sat beside her and rubbed Jess's arm. "What do you need?"

Jess groaned. "Stop being so nice."

"Sure, as soon as I know you're okay."

"I'm fine. I will be, anyway."

Ashley pulled a tissue out of her pocket and held it out. "You don't make it easy for me either, you know. I wouldn't give up Russ for anything, but the more time I spend with you, the more I think he was an idiot for letting you go."

"No, he wasn't." Jess took the tissue and dried her face. "He's great, but we got on each other's nerves. Honestly, I think I wanted to be part of the family more than I wanted to be with Russ. Besides, if it had worked out between us, you and I wouldn't have met."

"Is it weird that my husband's ex has become one of my best friends?"

"I am?"

Ashley shrugged. "I know. It's weird."

"It is, but ..." Jess didn't want to let on how much the admission meant to her.

"Let's not mention it again, okay?"

She smiled. "Deal."

"Now, will you tell me what's going on?"

Jess leaned back and braced herself. She told Ashley everything—about Felix's injury, his addiction, her mother's cheating and leaving, and her brother's relapse. By the time she finished, she was crying again. Ashley gave her another tissue. That simple gesture offered more comfort than Jess had felt in months, aside from Carter. "Thanks."

"Are you sure Felix relapsed? Maybe he's really sick."

"That's what Carter said."

Ashley perked up. "You and Carter have talked about this?"

"Turns out he's not too bad for a nerd. He's a good listener."

"Cute too."

"You're married. And pregnant."

"But you're not." Ashley waggled her eyebrows.

"No, I'm just the sister of an addict, the daughter of a cheater, and a head case in my own right."

"So?"

"You're not going to argue?" Jess didn't know how to feel about that.

Ashley grinned. "Russ said he broke up with you three times."

"Fair enough. It wasn't my finest hour."

"Maybe not, but you're not stuck there. Look at what you've done since then."

"I ran away from home like a grade-schooler."

"But you came back, and you took a really awkward job to help us out. Russ used to tense up whenever he talked about the business side of the farm. Ever since you started working here, he's relaxed. He trusts you completely."

"I didn't realize." How could she? "He trusts me? Really?"

"So do I, not that my opinion matters much when it comes to the farm."

Jess twisted the tissues in her hands, wanting to believe Ashley. "I don't know what to say."

"Because you're too busy looking back to see what's happening now, so stop it." Ashley sniffed. "I'm holding it together now, but my emotions are all over the place these days. Next time I might start crying with you."

Jess laughed. "It might be worth it to see that."

Ashley ripped the tissues out of her hand and tried to scowl, but she couldn't quite hide her smile. "Do it and I'll take back all the nice things I said. There weren't any witnesses."

"I can't imagine Russ wins many arguments with you."

"We haven't had many yet." A soft glow filled Ashley's cheeks.

"I hope it stays that way."

"Me too, but I'm too realistic to hold out for that."

"I'm sorry I distracted you." Jess wiped a finger under her eye to catch any stray mascara. "I'll let you get back to your work now."

Ashley's eyebrows creased. "What work?"

"Whatever it was you came here to do."

"Oh!" Her eyes widened as she smiled. "I had Russ drop me off so I could talk to you."

"How did you know I was here?"

"I saw your car when we drove by. You're working on *picnic* Saturday. You either forgot and needed me to remind you, or you're overworked and need help. Which is it?"

"Neither. I needed to finish up a few things, but I'm done now."

"Good." Ashley stood and pulled Jess to her feet. "Russ is running errands for Kathleen. No one's at the house yet. If we hurry, we can eat a pan of cinnamon rolls and dispose of the evidence before anyone realizes they're missing."

#

Jess moaned in delight as she popped the last bite of pastry into her mouth. "I thought you were joking. I can't believe we ate the whole pan."

Ashley scooped cream cheese frosting onto her finger, then licked it off. "I don't joke about baked goods. I barely thought about them before I got pregnant. Now I can barely think of anything else."

"At least you can blame it on the baby."

"I blame everything on her—naps, snacks, binge shopping."

"It's a girl?"

Ashley shrugged. "I won't know for a few weeks, but I didn't want to call her 'it' until we find out. Plus, Russ gets all nervous when he thinks of having a daughter. It's fun to torture him."

Jess picked up the empty pan and carried it to the sink. "You fed me. I'll clean up and hide the evidence."

The sliding glass door shooshed open. "Evidence of what?"

Jess glanced over at the sound of Russ's familiar baritone voice. While she looked at him, he looked at his wife, and everything in Jess's heart appreciated that. She turned on the water as inconspicuously as possible and turned her back to give them privacy.

"Whatcha washing?"

"She's helping me with breakfast dishes."

"We ate breakfast hours ago."

"Now it's time for the baby's breakfast."

"Right. Next time, make sure you don't have frosting on your lips when you tell that story."

"Jess!"

"What?" She glanced over her shoulder.

"You didn't tell me I had frosting on my lips."

"I wasn't looking at your lips." An instant revulsion—like watching her brother kiss his girlfriend—wormed its way into Jess's chest. "Ew. Get your mind out of the gutter, Russell."

He smiled. "A kiss from my wife is hardly the gutter."

As he leaned in, Jess turned back to the sink. It didn't take long to clean the pan and the few utensils she found there. She hoped that was enough time for Ashley and Russ to finish their make-out session.

Before she could turn around and check, a door banged open. "Russ, can you help Chad with the food?"

Russ's sister Rachel, followed by thunderous footsteps and a chorus of voices.

Jess wasn't sure where to go or what to do. She hadn't seen Rachel since the day they all showed up at this house after finding out about Russ's surprise engagement to a woman no one knew. That had been months ago, of course, and even though Jess and the sisters had been on the same side of disbelief back then, that didn't mean they'd be happy to see her again now, even if they knew why she was there.

"Do you mind?" Rachel, the middle sister, waddled into the kitchen, her pregnant belly entering a full three seconds before the rest of her. She held out a foil-covered pan.

"I don't mind at all." Jess took the pan, which smelled like berry crisp, but she couldn't take her eyes off Rachel's stomach.

Rachel smiled. "Two boys, due next month. I'm hoping to make it at least two more weeks."

"You look great."

"I feel like a beachball."

Ashley wrapped an arm around her sister-in-law and gave her a side hug. "I can't wait to meet them."

Russ and Chad carried boxes of food through the kitchen and out to the backyard. Jess mostly tried to stay out of everyone's way and helped with anything she could do one-handed while juggling the berry crisp. The other sisters, Carrie and Liz, arrived with their families before Kathleen returned carrying several full grocery sacks.

"Jessica." The older woman smiled. "Can you take this outside? Set it on the end of the food table."

With her arms full of paper products and dessert, Jess's body relaxed as she made her way outside. The midday sun heated the yard to above-normal temperatures, promising a pleasant afternoon for a picnic.

She'd just set the bag on the table when she spotted Carter's truck pulling around the side of the house. Curious, she waited and watched. He drove straight to where Russ stood. Once he'd stopped, a swarm of people lined up at the back of the truck and unloaded folding chairs. Unable to keep her curiosity at bay, she walked toward them. The instant Carter saw her, he smiled.

Her stomach fluttered. "Happy to see me?"

"Are you kidding? I don't think I have it in me to fend off another setup attempt."

Of course. What had she been thinking? "Where'd you find so many chairs?"

"The college. I had to put down a deposit, so don't even think about stealing one."

"Jess!" She turned to find Ashley waving from the house. "Can you give me a hand?"

"Do you want me to go?" Carter asked. "I can help inside if you have something you need to do here."

Something inside Jess went squishy. Carter was his normal, well-dressed self—which she could admit she found attractive—but it wasn't his appearance that turned her to jelly. What was wrong with her? Before she made a fool of herself in front of the Russell family again, she spun around and jogged toward the house. Ashley stood in the kitchen wringing her hands. "Is everything okay?" Jess asked.

Ashley grabbed her hand and pulled her through the crowded house to the front porch. As soon as the door closed, she said, "Kathleen doesn't know."

"Know what?"

She pointed at her stomach.

"You haven't told her?"

"I wanted to tell her in person two weeks ago, but we couldn't find a date when we were all available. Then, we were supposed to tell her last weekend, but I was so sick we cancelled the dinner. I was sick again Wednesday, so Russ was going to tell her, but he just told me that he didn't." Tears filled her eyes. "Someone's going to let it slip. I know it."

"Why don't you just pull her onto the porch and tell her?"

The tears rolled down Ashley's cheeks. "Because she's the only mom I get to tell, and I want it to be special. I know I'm being silly, but—" Her sobbing cut off the sentence.

Not sure what else to do, Jess wrapped her arms around Ashley and let her cry. "Do you think this might be pregnancy hormones?"

"I know it's pregnancy hormones." Jess's shoulder muffled Ashley's voice. "I tried to tell her inside, but I felt the tears coming. I don't want to cry when I tell her. I want to be happy."

"What about Russ?"

Ashley growled. An honest-to-goodness growl. "I wouldn't be crying about this now if he'd just remembered to tell her last week."

Jess patted Ashley's back with one hand. Just then Carter stepped around the side of the house, so she waved him away. He raised an eyebrow, then nodded before walking off.

Ashley's sobs turned to sniffles.

"Better?" Jess stepped back, trying to ignore the wet spot on her shirt.

"Yes, thank you." Ashley wiped her cheeks with the hem of her shirt. "I just needed to get the tears out, and I was afraid Russ's sisters would think I was crying about the baby or about Russ. I think I can tell her now."

"Ashley!" Russ's voice reached them before he did. He jumped onto the porch and pulled his wife into his arms. "What's wrong?"

Jess took that as her cue and tiptoed down the porch steps. By the time she made it to the back, dozens of banquet tables filled the yard. The smokey scent of barbecue floated through the air. People milled about, talking and laughing. She recognized almost everyone. To her surprise, all of them smiled at her as she walked by. As the new farm manager, she knew she should greet everyone and meet the people she didn't know yet, but she walked right to Carter as if she couldn't resist his pull.

He smiled when he saw her. "Everything okay?"

"Thanks for sending Russ."

He shrugged. "It looked like a situation he might want to know about."

"He sounded panicked when he showed up. What did you tell him?"

"That his wife was crying all over you on the porch."

Jess rolled her eyes. "That makes it sound like something terrible happened."

"How was I supposed to know it hadn't?"

"If it had been bad, I would have motioned you over."

"And how was I supposed to know *that*?"

Good question. "I don't know exactly, but I would've let you know somehow."

"Should I not have sent Russ?"

Jess's heart clenched at the uncertainty in his voice. "You're good. It was sweet to see how concerned Russ was. Come on." She smacked his arm and motioned toward the food tables. "Let's see if anyone needs help."

They walked across the lawn together, passing Chad along the way. Kathleen stepped onto the deck and yelled, "I knew it!" as Russ and Ashley followed her outside. The Russell siblings clapped and cheered, so Jess and Carter joined in. Russ wrapped one arm around Ashley as he signaled with the other for everyone to quiet down. It took several minutes for the noise to dwindle. When it did, Russ smiled.

"We're glad you all could join us this year and that the weather's cooperating. For those of you who haven't heard or figured it out yet"—he pulled Ashley closer as his smile stretched wider—"we're having a baby."

The yard erupted with applause, including Jess's. In fact, she couldn't contain her excitement for her friends.

Her friends. Not her ex and his wife. Her *friends*. The reality of that evolution nearly knocked the breath out of her.

"Why's everyone clapping?"

The familiar pitch of that voice choked out what little air remained in her lungs. Despite the warm sun, Jess shivered. Not wanting to cause a scene, she braced herself before turning around. "Angela."

"Angela? Honey, call me Mom."

Chapter Twelve

Her mother looked exactly as Jess expected her to look—blond hair almost to her waist, eyelashes for miles, and clothes practically painted onto her body. She hadn't always dressed that way, but it had become the norm in the months before she left.

"What are you doing here?" Jess asked.

"I brought Mom."

Jess's attention snapped to her grandmother, standing beside Carter. "I thought Dad was bringing you." But he was at the hospital with Felix. "I could have picked you up."

"It's okay. Angela stopped by, and she has a car." Gran smiled, but Jess recognized the tension in her lips and jaw.

"Will you excuse us?" Jess grabbed her mother's arm and pulled her across the yard. "You need to leave."

"Mom invited me to be her guest."

"This isn't Gran's party. It's the Russells'."

Her mom looked over her shoulder as Jess continued to pull her toward the house. "Who's that woman with Russ? I thought you two were serious."

"Are *you* serious?" Jess stopped walking to glare at her mother. "That was over two years ago. We broke up."

"Why?"

Because you made me crazy. Because I can't handle my problems any better than you can handle yours. A dozen other excuses ran through her mind, but Jess sighed before admitting the truth. "We weren't a good fit."

"Jessica." Gran's sweet voice softened her heart. Carter escorted her to where Jess and her mom stood. "I know this is a surprise, but I'd like it if Angela stayed."

"Why?"

"Because regardless of what's happened, she's still my daughter. We talked about this on the way over. Angela's going to eat with me, then she's going to leave. You can drive me home."

Anger, frustration, and anxiety raced through Jess's veins. "Fine. I'll eat with Carter."

Her mother frowned. "Jessica—"

"If that doesn't work for you, I can make a plate to go and meet Dad at home."

"Don't do that." Her mom took Gran's hand. "I'll eat and leave. I promise."

Jess nodded—not that her mother's word meant much to her anymore. "Thank you for bringing Gran. I appreciate it." Her mom smiled, but Gran led her away before she could say anything else. Jess sighed.

"So ... that's your mom?"

"Yep."

"Are you okay?"

"Nope."

"Wanna skip the food table and go straight to the dessert table?"

Jess rolled her eyes. "Do you really think dessert is all a woman needs to fix her relationship problems?"

"Of course not. You could probably use some therapy and a few self-help classes, but there's a giant carrot cake over there that looks amazing, and I'd like to get a piece before it's gone." He offered his arm. Still the gentleman.

She smiled, wrapped her arm around his biceps, and leaned into him. "I never know what to expect from you."

He led her toward the desserts. "Is that a good thing?"

"It's just an observation. It's fun, though."

They were the first people at the dessert table, and they walked away with a piece of carrot cake, a brownie, peanut butter marshmallow rice squares, three different cookies, and a promise to share everything so they could sample as many things as possible. Avoiding Jess's mom turned out to be surprisingly easy. Between introducing Carter to the rest of Russ's family, eating lunch, and helping Rachel so she didn't have to stand up any more than necessary, Jess almost forgot about her mom.

Then Dad arrived.

His already haggard face seemed to droop when he noticed his wife. He had enough to worry about with Felix. Jess wouldn't let her mom drag him down any further. Not caring what anyone said or thought, she excused herself and marched to her mom.

"Time's up." She picked up Mom's purse and grabbed her elbow. "I'll walk you to your car."

"But I'm not—"

Jess leaned close and lowered her voice. "You're done. I don't want to make a scene, but I will."

Gran wiped her mouth with a shaky hand. "That was a lovely meal, but I think I'm ready to go home. Angela, will you drive me?"

Her mom stood, but Jess didn't let go of her arm. Instead, she pulled her away from her dad and took the long way around the house.

Her mom stiffened. "Your father's here."

"I know."

"I'd like to say hello." She tried to change course, but Jess tightened her grip.

"Not here. You can call him later."

"I have called. He's never home."

Jess snorted.

"What?"

"Where do you think he goes? It's not like he joined a knitting club. Maybe he's ignoring your calls."

Her mom stumbled.

Jess stopped long enough for her to regain her balance. And to see the frown on her mother's face. "What's wrong?"

"I just ... I didn't ..." She twisted her arm away from Jess. "You don't need to manhandle me. And I don't need an escort."

"Maybe not, but it makes me feel better."

Her mom's frown deepened. "I raised you better than to be intentionally cruel."

A few heads turned toward them. Jess started walking again. "You're not really in a position to take the moral high ground." Not wanting to discuss it further, she picked up the pace until they rounded the house and stepped out of sight. She wasn't sure what her mom drove, so she stopped at the edge of the makeshift parking lot. Her mom managed to safely cross the rest of the lawn in her wedge sandals. "I'll go get Gran. You get your car."

Before she could move, however, Carter escorted Gran around the house. Jess's dad followed a few steps behind. After months of apologizing and getting involved in the community, her hard work and reputation-repair efforts were one Miller-family feud away from being flushed down the drain. Why couldn't her family just stay home? Gran, Carter, and her parents stood beside her, squaring off for the first time in years.

"Angela." Her dad nodded.

"Cliff."

"I didn't know you were in town."

"I called, but you never answer."

He scratched the back of his head and winced. "I thought it was a telemarketer."

"I left messages."

He chuckled. "I never check those. Why'd you call?"

"I wanted to talk. I think we owe each other that." Her mom at least had the decency to blush.

"How long are you in town? Maybe we can talk next week."

Jess clenched her jaw. "Why would you talk to her?"

He patted her arm. "It's okay, Smooch. There's no need to be angry until we know if there's a reason to be angry."

"Of course there's a reason to be angry."

Her mom looked around. "Why can't we talk now?"

"I need to get back to the hospital."

Jess sucked in a breath. How could she forget? "How is he?"

"Recovering. His appendix ruptured. They had to do an emergency appendectomy, but everything went well. He needs to stay overnight though."

Relief and guilt swept over Jess. "He didn't relapse." Tears rushed down her face. When an arm wrapped around her, she didn't hesitate to turn into Carter's hug.

"What happened? Who are you talking about?" Her mother's grating voice couldn't squelch the joy of Felix's sobriety.

Her dad updated her mom and Gran as Jess leaned into Carter's support.

"Are you okay?" he whispered near her ear.

She nodded.

"You sure? Because I'm pretty sure you're shaking."

"I thought that was you."

When he chuckled, his chest rumbled. Everything about it—the warmth, the tone, and the gentle vibration—soothed her overworked nerves. She needed to step away, to go with her dad, but she didn't trust her legs to carry her to her car, much less get her to the hospital. She couldn't ask Carter to drive her though, not now that she'd finally convinced people she wasn't such a wreck. With that in mind, she stepped out of his embrace. "Thanks for that, but I should get to the hospital."

"Want to come with me?" her dad asked.

"I'll drive myself. I'd like to stay with him for a while, and I don't want you to have to wait for me." She glared at her mom. "No, you can't go. I'll tell Felix you're in town. If he wants to see you, I'll text Gran. If he doesn't, then you stay away. He doesn't need an excuse to jump off the wagon."

Her mom opened her mouth, but Gran lifted a hand. "Jessica's right. Felix has made a lot of progress. He gets to decide what he can and can't handle."

"I'm his *mother*. I should be there for him."

"That's enough, Ang." Her dad's voice didn't waiver. "We can talk about this after you take Dot home."

Her mom's jaw quivered. Jess braced herself for a tantrum, but her mom merely stomped off toward a tan sedan.

Gran sighed. "I don't know what I did wrong with her."

"Mom's not your fault." Jess pulled Gran in for a sideways hug. "She made her own decisions."

"Still …" Gran shook her head. "I pray for that girl every night. And I'll be praying for Felix too. You call me before you leave the hospital, okay?"

"I promise."

Gran made her way to the sedan. Dad kissed Jess's cheek, then hopped into his truck. Jess turned to thank Carter one more time and froze. Kathleen and Russ watched her from the side of the house. So much for progress.

Forcing a smile, she gave Carter her full attention. "I need to get to the hospital."

"Are you okay to drive?"

She nodded because she didn't trust her voice.

He wrapped his fingers around hers. "What's wrong?"

Too much to mention, so she said, "I'm proud of Felix. I hope he can forgive me for doubting him." And that the Russells would forget the past few minutes, though that was probably too much to ask.

Chapter Thirteen

The hospital doors slid apart, welcoming Jess to a foyer she'd hoped to never see again. Instrumental music filtered through the cold, white space as sunshine shone through the skylights in the cathedral ceiling. She doubted she'd ever like visiting the hospital, but at least this time she wasn't dreading her conversation with the doctor.

She spotted her dad as soon as she stepped inside. He smiled at her from his seat beside the welcome desk, standing as she approached him. "You got here fast," she said, pulling him into a hug.

"I've only been here about fifteen seconds. I wanted to be here in case you need me."

"Where is he?"

"Fourth floor." He led her through familiar territory to her brother's room. They stopped outside the open door. Felix lay on the inclined bed covered by a too-small hospital blanket, an IV in his arm and his eyes closed.

Jess grabbed Dad's hand. "How long does he have to stay here?"

"At least twenty-four hours. Longer if he has issues."

"What about the pain meds?"

"We explained everything to the emergency room doctor. They used a non-opioid anesthesia and can give him less addictive pain meds."

Hope forced more tears into her eyes. "So he won't relapse?"

"Hopefully not. He asked me to call his sponsor before he went into surgery. He's going to swing by the hospital tomorrow so they can talk with the doctor and come up with a plan to help Felix heal and keep him clean." He nudged her with his arm. "Go see him. He asked me to bring you back. I'll talk to him when you're done."

Her heart fluttered with equal parts anxiety and relief as she stepped into the darkened room. She tried not to disturb Felix, but as she reached the end of the bed he said, "You smell like barbecue."

"Sorry."

"Don't apologize. It's delicious." He opened his eyes and smiled. "Thanks for coming."

She rushed to his side and carefully picked up his hand. "I'm so sorry I doubted you. I need you to know that."

"Don't apologize." He squeezed her fingers. "You were right to doubt me."

"I'm glad Dad didn't. I would have dropped you at the door and driven away." Jess sank onto the chair beside him but kept ahold of his hand. "How are you feeling?"

"I'm thankful for laparoscopic surgery. The incisions are small."

"Do they hurt?"

"A little, but it's nothing serious. I'd rather have a little discomfort and no oxycodone."

"You're sure you can handle it?" What if he tried to be a hero and backslid instead?

"My sponsor is coming tomorrow to help me with that. He broke his ankle a few years ago and had to have surgery. He worked with the doctors to manage the pain and stay sober. He's going to help me track my meds."

"I'll help too. Just let me know what to do. I am *so* proud of you."

He started to smile, but his lips stretched into a wide yawn. "Sorry. I'm still a little groggy."

"I'll let you rest, but Dad wants to talk to you first."

Felix's gaze drifted over her head. "Everything okay?"

She looked over her shoulder. Her dad stood right behind her. He set a hand on her shoulder and squeezed. "Your mother's in town," he said. "She wants to see you."

"Why?"

"I didn't ask."

"Does it matter?" Jess asked, her chest tightening. "She left."

"But she came back. She must have a reason." Felix yawned again, his eyes fluttering closed before he snapped them open. "I'll talk to my sponsor about it tomorrow. Tell her I'll call her when I'm ready."

"But—" Jess wanted to argue, but her dad squeezed her shoulder again. Her mind scrambled. "Maybe ... tomorrow is too soon. Take as much time as you need." Felix nodded, but his eyes stayed shut. Jess kissed his hand before releasing it and walking out of the room with her dad. "Should one of us stay with him tonight?"

"He'll be fine, Smooch. He'll probably sleep all night anyway."

"I guess." But that didn't mean she had to feel good about it. "Maybe I'll bring Gran over before and after church tomorrow."

"I think he'd appreciate that. Until then, why don't you go back to your party? Now that you've seen your brother, you can relax and enjoy yourself."

She slipped her arm through his and led him to the elevator. "I don't know if that's possible. I've spent so much time trying to prove to the Russells that I've got my life together, then Mom showed up." She pressed the down button. "I don't know if I have the energy to start over again."

The elevator pinged as the doors slid open. Inside stood Russ, Ashley, and Carter. Jess tensed.

"Are you okay?" Ashley rushed out and pulled Jess into a breath-stopping hug. "Carter told us about your brother. How is he?"

"I'll see you at home." Jess's dad winked before stepping into the elevator. "I won't wait up for you."

Jess pried herself from Ashley's grasp. "He's good. He's sleeping now, but he might get to go home tomorrow. Why are you here?"

Ashley's eyes widened. "Are you kidding? We wanted to make sure you were okay. Kathleen wanted to come too, but Russ convinced her to stay at the picnic to keep things running."

"But ..." Jess looked between the faces of the three people in front of her. "I don't understand. Why?"

Ashley glanced at Russ. He wrapped an arm around her before focusing on Jess. "You're practically family. We couldn't enjoy ourselves if you were here alone."

The warmth and comfort of his sentiment wrapped around her, but she couldn't let herself embrace it. She knew the calm wouldn't last. "But my mom ... just because there wasn't a scene this time doesn't mean there won't be."

Russ snorted. "If we kicked out every person who'd ever made a scene at a family function, I'd never see my sisters again. Or my mom. Most of the nephews."

Ashley elbowed him. "Remember Kristy's tantrum at Christmas?"

"Epic."

Jess rolled her eyes. "She's a baby."

"There was a lot of screaming," Russ said.

Ashley nodded. "And projectile sweet potatoes."

Despite her efforts not to, Jess smiled. "You're just trying to make me feel better."

"Of course we are," Ashley said. "Today was a hard day for you. We want to make it better, if we can."

Jess didn't know what to say, especially when her gaze shifted away from the Russells and onto Carter. With his hands in his pockets and his shoulders casually set, he reminded her of a catalog model, except he wasn't smiling as he watched her. The tight set of his jaw and pressed line of his mouth spoke of his concern.

She stepped toward him. "You told on me."

He shrugged. "I know how you see yourself, but you're the only one who feels that way. I figured Russ and Ashley would want to know what was going on."

"How could you possibly know that? I didn't even know that."

He shrugged again. "I'm a good listener."

He sure was. She'd expected him to be like every other guy she'd ever met, but he continued to surprise her. What surprised her even more was the tenderness he stirred in her. She doubted he'd ever be the country boy she usually dated—did he even own work boots? She never thought she'd swap romance novels with a guy or want to know what hair product he used to achieve such effortless-looking style. Most guys asked for her number or propositioned her or, in Russ's case, picked her brain for information, but Carter didn't fit into any of those molds. She didn't understand him, but that didn't scare her. It warmed the tenderness he stirred in her until the discomfort of it stoked a new, unfamiliar realization in her heart.

She was crazy about him.

She'd been wrong about needing to prove herself to the Russells. Maybe—hopefully—she'd been wrong about staying single too.

Carter cocked his head to the side. "Are you okay? You look a little constipated."

Ignoring his attempt to make her smile, she made her move. Jess leaned into him and tilted her lips up.

He stepped back, eyes wide.

Humiliation slammed into her like a combine. "Oh, God." Before she said or did anything else stupid, she ran for the stairs.

"Jess!"

She ignored them, not trusting herself not to break down in front of them. As she shoved open the fireproof door, a dozen accusations whirled through her brain.

How could she be so stupid? Carter had never expressed interest in dating her. He'd never even asked for her phone number! Was she so self-centered, so out of touch with reality, that she assumed every man wanted to date her? Why did she have to do that in front of Russ and Ashley? How long would it take her to find a new job, and would Texas be far enough away that she could hide forever?

By the time she reached the ground floor, tears covered her cheeks and her heart raced, more from embarrassment than from the impromptu workout. Pulling a tissue out of her purse, she took a minute to relax and collect herself. Once her face was dry and her breathing had calmed, she opened the door and stepped into the lobby.

"Why did you run away?" Carter stood in the lobby looking as casual and relaxed as he had upstairs.

Her gut clenched. "What are you doing here?"

"Waiting for you."

"Why?"

"Because you didn't give me a chance to recover."

"That's why I ran. You can recover. I can recover. We can pretend like that never happened."

Casual Carter disappeared as he stepped in front of her and wrapped an arm around her waist. "I don't think we're on the same page." His free hand traced the curve of her jaw.

Jess's heart fluttered at the sweetness of the touch. "I don't think we're in the same book. What are you doing?"

"You are so far out of my league that I never imagined you'd be interested in me." He looked into her eyes as his smile widened. "You're a brilliant, beautiful woman with a history of dating men who are the complete opposite of me, but the more time we spent together, the further I fell down the rabbit hole. You were always so cool and collected, while it took everything in me not to ruin everything by asking you out."

The arm around her waist tightened. She wanted to believe him, but, "You stepped back."

His chest rumbled with laughter. "You shocked the daylights out of me. I thought *I* was the one misreading things. I moved because I couldn't believe you were trying to kiss me."

"Are you kidding me?" She cupped his smooth cheeks with her palms, enamored with their unfamiliar yet intoxicating texture. "You're the sexiest nerd I've ever met." Knowing she'd never find words as sweet as Carter's, she pulled his face to hers and kissed him.

His arms tightened around her as he kissed her back. She shifted in his embrace, letting his soapy, masculine scent seep into her as she reveled in his touch. Why had she avoided this for so long?

"Would you look at that?" Gran's voice cut through the hospital chatter.

Jess stepped back—reluctantly—as she tried to come up with an excuse for her very public display of affection. Carter let her have her space, but he wove his fingers between hers. Heat engulfed her ears. Her dad and Gran approached them from the front door.

Gran grinned as she walked up to Jess and hugged her. "You had me worried, sweetheart, but I knew you'd come around."

"You knew I'd kiss Carter in the hospital lobby?"

She chuckled as she stepped back. "I knew you'd stop worrying about everyone else and get back to living your life. Eventually."

"Why does everyone else seem to know more about my life than I do?"

"Because we care more about *you* than how you fit in and who you fit in with."

Carter squeezed her hand. "You fit in well with us. Who else do you need?"

Who else, indeed.

"That was quite the kiss," someone stage-whispered from behind them. Jess spun around. Ashley and Russ stood there, smiling.

"Where did you come from?"

Ashley shrugged. "We come. We go. We're heading back to the picnic now. I wanted to make sure you're coming, right?"

To an afternoon outside with her family and friends? Jess tugged on Carter's hand, pulling him next to her so she could lean against him. "As long as we don't have to talk about dead people."

Did you miss Practically Married?

Read chapter one now!

This is Tom, please leave a message.

Ashley disconnected, unwilling to leave another voicemail. Tom had promised to check his messages during his hiking trip, but that was ten days ago. He must've had a signal at some point since then. How could an entire section of Michigan function without phones? Unless something had happened to him. She stared into the living room, tapping her fingers on the Formica table, her nails clicking in time with the scenarios flying through her head. Her aunt and uncle's afghan-covered furniture and beige, contractor-grade carpet offered little counsel.

The bedroom door squeaked behind her. "Good heavens, you're up early, sweetheart. Is everything okay?" Rose managed to sound chipper despite the hour.

"I couldn't sleep. I still can't reach Tom." Ashley spun the useless phone on the table.

Rose patted her shoulder on the way to the kitchen. "Maybe you should postpone the move, at least until you hear from Tom. You're welcome to stay with John and me until then."

"Thanks, but I'm ready to go. In all fairness, Tom warned me I might not be able to reach him, but I didn't expect total radio silence." In the kitchen, cupboards thudded, dishes clinked, and silverware rattled. When Rose finally returned, her pink shirt glowed behind a short stack of butter-yellow plates and glistening silverware. "Do you usually set the table for breakfast?" Ashley asked.

"Of course not, but you don't usually join us either. Are you sure you don't want to go back to sleep for a while? It's barely eight."

Ashley laughed. "I'll survive, though I don't think I've set my alarm this early since high school."

Her aunt set down the plates, then grabbed Ashley's hand and gave it a squeeze. "That was a lifetime ago, wasn't it?"

Ashley nodded. The pain had dulled, but the reality of her parents' deaths never disappeared. "Living my entire adult life without Mom and Dad isn't how I would have planned things, but it's worked out. I can't imagine life without you and Uncle John at every turn."

"We've gotten spoiled." Rose kissed the top of Ashley's head. "I'm not excited about sharing you with anyone, especially someone who's not as crazy about you as we are."

"No one will ever be as crazy about me as you are, but Tom and I are great friends. Mom always said she was glad she married her best friend. I think she'd be happy that I found someone like him."

"Maybe. Are you sure you want to spend your life with a man who would marry a woman he's never met?"

"It's not like we're complete strangers. We text and talk all the time, plus we video chat, which at least lets us see each other."

Rose shook her head, her long, silver hair swaying around her shoulders. "I'm glad I met John before all your world-wide Google dating. There's nothing more romantic than a handwritten love letter. Now, what would you like for breakfast?"

"Why don't I make breakfast for you today?" Ashley hopped up. "What would you like?"

"Do you know how to make breakfast? I thought you only woke up for lunch." Rose winked before heading into the white-tiled kitchen.

Ashley followed, missing her already. "I hope I'm still full of sass when I'm seventy-five. Sometimes I wonder how much trouble you and Mom would have gotten into if she was still here."

"I wouldn't get into any trouble. I had a way of tricking your mom into making all the bad decisions."

Ashley's laughter mingled with her aunt's—the same tone, but decades older. They worked side-by-side, whipping up eggs and chopping vegetables.

"Could you reach my serving bowl on the top shelf there?" Rose pointed to the far cabinet.

Ashley pulled a blue ceramic dish from above the microwave. "Did you buy a stepladder for when I'm gone?"

"Nonsense. John can reach it for me."

"And what if he's gone?"

"Where would he go without me? He's eighty years old."

A deep chuckle rumbled through the kitchen. "Eighty's the new sixty." Ashley turned and smiled at her uncle as he toweled his hair in the bedroom doorway, his blue eyes twinkling in the morning light. "What in the world are you doing up?" he asked. "I wasn't expecting to see you until noon."

"My flight's at noon, Uncle John. We need to leave for the airport by ten."

"Good grief, that's a long time to hang out at the airport. Why don't you stay with us for a while longer?"

"Your retirement community doesn't allow thirty-five-year-olds to live here."

"Ah, they're old. Mumble when you talk to them. They won't understand, but they'll be too embarrassed to ask you to repeat yourself."

Ashley laughed, but she appreciated the sentiment. "I think it's time for me to move on, don't you?"

"What do I know? I'm an old man." John walked over and wrapped an arm around her. "I want you to be happy, even if that means moving to the tundra." He shivered as he said the word. "I can't imagine why you want to move there in November, but I don't understand much about how you do things these days."

Ashley leaned into him, happy to reassure him again. "Lots of people meet online. Tom's a good man. We have the same values, and we make each other laugh. We'll be good for each other."

"Bleh." Rose wrinkled her nose. "This isn't an arranged marriage. You can take time to date and fall in love."

Ashley cringed. "Love doesn't always last. Tom's sister and one of his cousins married for love, but they fell out of love, divorced, and remarried. Tom and I have a lot in common, including our frustration with dating. We're tired of being alone, and we're committed to making it work.

"My mom and dad were friends who fell in love and got married. Tom and I will be friends who get married, then fall in love." Hopefully. Returning phone calls might speed up the falling-in-love process. "Besides, I have to move now. The photographer I told you about is expecting me to start my internship after New Year's. I want to be there early so I can get settled."

Rose scooped eggs into the serving bowl. "You take beautiful pictures already. Why do you need an internship?"

"Because I'm not good enough yet to make a living at it. I've only been able to sell a few landscapes and still-life photos, but if I can learn how to take portraits, too, I could make a decent career for myself as a photographer."

John shook his head. "Why do you need to make a career for yourself? You're getting married."

Ashley rolled her eyes. "Yes, and I can have a career too. This isn't the Teddy Roosevelt era anymore."

He tugged on Ashley's hair. "You have my blessing to go now."

"That's all I've ever wanted." She let herself lean against him a while longer, soaking in his support and love, as she had for the last decade and a half. His spring-fresh scent mixed with the savory aroma of her aunt's sizzling sausage, the same brand Ashley's mom used to cook. "I think Mom would've liked Tom."

Rose turned to her. "Are you still reading through her journal? Haven't you memorized it by now?"

Ashley glanced at the worn blue notebook on the dining-room table. "I only found it two years ago. I never realized how much Mom supported me. Even when she wanted me to take more English classes in high school, she encouraged me in math and started researching possible engineering careers for me."

What would her mom think now, knowing Ashley lived in the same house she grew up in, working out of the living room as a medical transcriptionist? Not the life Mom had written about for her only daughter, but Ashley was changing that. She would make her mom proud. "The one thing Mom wrote consistently about was being a grandma someday. Did you know she had given up on having kids a year before she found out she was pregnant with me?"

Rose chuckled as she rushed around the kitchen dishing up food. "I remember the day she found out. I went to the doctor with her. We thought it would be a quick stop, then we were going shoe shopping. That doctor said 'pregnant,' and we bought half the baby clothes in JCPenney. When your daddy came home, he stared at your mom like he didn't know where babies came from."

Rose told the rest of the story—the baby shower, the delivery, the crying—as Ashley set the table. By the time Rose finished, she'd piled food onto each plate. As they sat down, Ashley's stomach rumbled.

John patted her hand. "Why don't you go ahead and call that boyfriend of yours? I'll feel better dropping you off at the airport if I know he's going to meet you on the other side."

Ashley picked up her phone from the table and stuffed it in her pocket. "He's still out of range, but I've left him a few voicemails. I'm sure Tom will be there."

#

The phone rang again, the obnoxious chirp echoing through the house. Russ took his time walking down the stairs, fastening the last button of his oxford before tucking it into his jeans. Thick cotton socks muffled his slow steps. No reason to rush. He had no idea what he'd say if he answered the phone anyway.

At the base of the stairs, he caught sight of his reflection in the glass covering an old family picture. Dark eyes stared back at him. Mom would ask him to cut his hair when she saw him—the curls were popping out again. She wouldn't mention the beard. Though she hated it, she'd been losing that battle for twenty years. Tom had always kept a clean face. Her baby-faced nephew.

A familiar pain pressed against Russ' chest. He didn't have time for that. His family would start arriving soon. He glanced at the clock behind him, the second hand ticking in front of pictures of Tom's favorite northern birds. Any minute now the front door would open, but the phone kept chirping.

By the time Russ reached the dining room, the ringing stopped. He pulled the phone out of the hutch drawer. *Ashley* flashed across the screen an instant before the phone beeped. Another voicemail. If he had the passcode, he could find out who she was and why she kept calling, but he didn't have the strength to talk to her anyway. She'd been calling for two days, though. He really should call her back. Later. After he figured out what to say.

The front door groaned. A hundred footsteps thundered against the hardwood in the foyer. Two soft steps padded toward him. Russ smiled. He tossed the phone back in the drawer and looked up as three-year-old Phin plowed into him.

The typically unrestrained boy wrapped his arms around Russ' legs, his blue eyes wide and wet. "Mama cwying."

Russ scooped up the little guy. "I know, bud. Uncle Russ cried a little bit too."

That innocent face brightened. "You did?"

"I did."

"You cwy now?"

"I'll try not to. We'll leave that to your mom and aunts."

"Aunt Wiz cwy?" Phin's bottom lip trembled.

Oh no.

Rachel and Chad ushered their other boys into the adjoining, open-concept kitchen. Russ couldn't be responsible for making her baby cry. Holding Phin out in front of him, he tossed the boy in the air.

"Again!" Phin squealed as his older brothers ran at Russ.

"Me too!"

"My turn!"

Their dad pulled them away, throwing one over his shoulder and tucking one under his arm as if wrangling six-and eight-year-olds were easy. "We'll let Mommy talk to Uncle Russ. Let's find you a movie." More squeals and cheering filled the room as Phin squirmed out of Russ' arms to run away with his brothers. That left Rachel and Russ alone, staring at each other, the loneliness of the house closing in around them.

Tears rolled down Rachel's cheeks. "I'm so sorry."

"It's not your fault, Rach." She nodded but didn't stop crying. He pulled her into a hug, summoning all of his remaining strength for her to absorb. "Thanks for coming over."

She nodded, wiping her tears and nose on him. Maybe he should have worn a work shirt instead of his church shirt. The door opened again, followed by more footsteps, voices, and the throaty cry of his only niece.

Rachel stepped back, squeezing Russ' hand. "Carrie was right behind me, and I think I saw Liz pulling in too. You go greet everyone. I'll get the food out."

"I don't have any food."

She laughed as she walked into the kitchen.

Russ moved through the randomly furnished living room. A fire popped in the cobblestone fireplace, throwing soft, warm light onto the mismatched couch, loveseat, and oversized chair. Before he made it to the foyer, his oldest nephew jumped onto the chair, his feet dangling over the arm while he fiddled with his phone. Russ walked toward the front door, but a pile of coats and boots blocked his path.

Liz looked at him, her young eyes red and tired. "The diaper bag spilled in the car, and I can't find Kristy's snacks. Do you have anything she can eat?" She passed off the crying infant to Russ. "I'll nurse her in a bit, but I need to clean up the mess and see if I can find that tube of rice puffs for her."

"How about yogurt?" The one thing he stocked especially for Kristy. That little girl owned his heart like his three sisters never had. He was pretty confident the feeling was mutual. Kristy dropped her bald head onto his shoulder, grabbed the dry half of his collar, and stuffed it into her mouth. He turned back toward the kitchen, but someone grabbed his elbow and steered him around.

Liz hugged him. "How are you doing?"

He wrapped his free arm around her. "The house is quiet."

"We can take care of that for a few hours." His youngest sister held him tighter than Rachel had but without the tears. "Thanks for letting us come over."

"Like I had a choice."

She smacked his chest before walking back outside.

Russ stepped over the great coat divide, passed the staircase in the foyer, and trekked into the family room. Little boys covered the sectional. Five nephews aged three to twelve climbed over and around each other as a cartoon played on the flat screen. Their dads talked in the corner, one facing the kids while one watched the kitchen. Russ walked by them, nodding as he passed. They offered the same salute.

As soon as he stepped onto the gray kitchen tiles, Rachel and Carrie stopped talking. Somehow, they'd covered the island countertop with food. They removed lids and foil from pots and pans. Buttery, garlicky aromas floated through the air. Rachel rushed over to steal Kristy, but the baby burrowed into Russ' neck.

He smiled at Rachel's fake hurt expression. "Could you get her something to eat?" he asked.

She nodded, her eyes still pink and puffy. Their oldest sister, Carrie, walked over, squeezing him and Kristy in a quick, tearless hug. He could always count on her for emotional stability. Carrie was the closest person he had to a brother, besides Tom.

"How are you doing?" she asked. "Can I get you anything?"

"Shouldn't I be asking you that? This is my house."

"Yes, but you're a man. We brought our own comfort food."

His stomach growled. "What kind of comfort?"

Carrie grinned. "Mom's bringing the pie."

Russ salivated. Mom's comfort always came baked between two perfectly flaky crusts. "I hope it's apple."

"She's probably bringing pumpkin, cherry, blueberry, *and* apple."

"She trained us. You know there'll be too much food." Rachel returned with a bowl of banana pieces.

"I don't mind at all." Russ took the bowl and sat at the large oak table with Kristy on his lap. He gave her one piece at a time, the way his sisters had taught him.

Chatter and laughter filled the old farmhouse, warming it in a way the fireplace never could. Carrie's husband stepped into the kitchen and snagged some food, taking a moment to wrap his arms around her and kiss her hair. Two boys stormed through the house laughing and yelling. They charged toward the dining room and right into Rachel. Blessed chaos.

Something warm and wet pressed on Russ' hand. He looked down at Kristy, eyes closed, head resting on his hand, and drool rolling down onto the table. Her tiny pink shirt stretched and contracted with her rapid baby breaths.

Russ hadn't wanted his family over. He'd thought he needed time to process, to let reality sink in, but having them there was what he really needed. He would never understand how his sisters realized that about him, but he liked it. Maybe not the drool, but everything else he liked.

Another whoosh of air caught his attention. Russ leaned back, trying to see through the living room and its walls to the front door. A puffy purple sleeve swung into the foyer. Mom.

She and Liz marched toward him balancing pie plates on their hands. If they ever showed up wearing the same outfit, it would be like watching past and present versions of the same woman. Carrie met them midway, taking all three pies to the kitchen.

Russ' mom stepped behind his chair and wrapped her arms around him. "You are a wonderful man, Edgar James Russell. I'm so proud to have you as a son."

Her words strangled his heart. He forced down tears and nodded. "Thanks, Mom. How're Aunt Rita and Uncle Bill?"

She walked around the table and sat across from him. "They're doing okay. The girls came home this week, so at least the family's together. They asked about you. You were closer to Tommy than either of his sisters, and they wanted to make sure you're okay. I can't imagine losing a son, especially this close to the holidays."

Liz set a plate of food in front of Russ before scooping up Kristy. "Thanks. Do you want anything, Mom?"

"No, I'm fine."

Liz took an empty plate from the island and set it in front of their mom. "Just in case."

Russ watched his family roam around. They didn't ask anything of him, didn't make him talk. It wouldn't last long. Rachel would eventually come up with her thousand questions, but for now she respected his space. He ignored his plate and simply enjoyed watching them. His little sisters, all grown up. Wives and mothers. Three great men who loved them, wrangling kids in the other room. All of them giving him the support he needed. Until they left. Then he'd be alone again. He'd never envied his sisters' marriages until now.

He didn't have time to worry about that, though. The farm needed constant attention, and Russ would have to work for two people next year. Starting his own family would have to wait awhile. None of the women in the kitchen would like that, but he couldn't control everything.

Besides, he had two more years before he hit forty. Plenty of time. Two years to find a woman more interested in a marriage than a wedding, someone committed to as-long-as-they-both-shall-live, not simply as-long-as-the-romance-stays-alive. Maybe two years wouldn't be long enough, but right now he only wanted to—needed to—appreciate his family. Nothing else mattered.

Chad sauntered into the kitchen, his large frame dwarfing the women as he passed. He pulled out the chair beside Russ and dropped onto the seat. "We need to talk about the farm."

Meet the Novak Sisters

Here's a sneak peek at book one, *Finally Forever*!

The crisp manilla folder taunted Caroline as she stepped into her office. She flipped on the light before setting her briefcase-sized purse on the floor. The leather chair squeaked under her weight as she picked up the file.

ORIENTATION.

Not her favorite way to start the week. Opening the folder, she scanned the list of new hires as the sun warmed her through the third-story window. She recognized a few names, but one made her pause. Ben Allen. It couldn't be. She flipped through his paperwork.

Football player at Western Michigan University. Degree in business analytics with a minor in accounting. Graduate of Traverse City Central High School. All-American defensive end. No doubt about it, he was the same Ben Allen who had graduated with her younger sister Christine.

"Good morning, Caroline."

She looked up to find her boss standing in the doorway, casual as ever in khakis and a short-sleeved button-down shirt. "Morning, John. I was just looking through the file you left me."

"That's why I stopped over." He smiled, his fatherly face crinkling. When he shut the door, Caroline perked up. John Marsh rarely needed to discuss confidential things with her. If he felt the need to close the door, she was going to give him her full attention. "I suppose you recognized Ben Allen's name."

"I did."

"Then you know he's a bit of a celebrity."

An understatement. "Division one football players usually are. I was surprised to see his name. I didn't realize he'd moved home."

John sat in one of the chairs across from her. "Not many people know. Ben and the family have been quiet about it. They weren't even sure he'd come home until his father spoke with Al."

"Al Morrison?" Owner and founder of the company? Interesting.

"A friend of the Allens. After physical therapy, they wanted him to come home, but he was hesitant. Al wasn't. He offered the kid a job as soon as he read Ben's résumé."

Caroline's heart cracked a little. She couldn't imagine settling for insurance work after training for the NFL. It had to be hard for a twenty-three-year-old to process. "I'll find him a good mentor. I was thinking of—"

"I want you to be his mentor."

"Excuse me?" Her heart tightened as she glanced at the folders still in her purse.

"I need someone who won't be starstruck."

"I don't mentor anymore." And she had no desire to start, even for a celebrity.

"Just this once. You'll be able to work with him objectively. Teach him the ropes without getting distracted. You'll be perfect." John tapped the desk twice before standing. His unofficial sign-off. "Ben will be here later today. Meet me in my office at one. He'll start orientation next week with everyone else."

Without another word, John disappeared. Panic swirled in Caroline's mind and throat as she imagined her free time disappearing. Needing the comfort of a familiar voice, she grabbed the phone and dialed Chris.

"Caro, what's wrong? Why are you calling?" her sister asked.

"Did you know Ben is working at Morrison?"

"You interrupted my PE class for this?"

"My boss wants me to be his mentor. I'm not sure how to keep press, stalkers, and groupies out of the office." And she doubted the mentoring stipend was adequate compensation for the hassle.

Chris laughed. "Don't be dramatic. No one will know he's there. He's been pretty quiet since the injury. Now, stop calling me at work unless it's an *actual* emergency."

The line went dead, and Caroline sighed. Chris was right. Sure, Ben was the biggest celebrity Traverse City had ever produced, but it was only Traverse City. Population fourteen thousand. She doubted there were enough professional photographers in the whole county to make up a respectable group of paparazzi. And maybe it wouldn't be that bad. If Ben wanted a quiet life, Morrison would be the perfect place. There wasn't much about the classic car insurance company that would remind him of football *or* attract a fan base.

***

Ben checked his reflection in the window. He'd driven past the Morrison Insurance building dozens of times in his life, but this would be his first time inside. Unfortunately, it wouldn't be his last. If he thought about it too long, he'd want to put his fist through the glass, so he pushed the temptation aside. Time to face reality.

He opened the door, and a cool blast of air washed over him. A nice-looking woman smiled at him from behind the receptionist's desk. With her chin-length gray-blonde hair, wire-frame glasses, and bright lipstick, she reminded him of his aunt.

"Good afternoon. How can I help you?" she asked.

"I'm Ben Allen. I'm here to see John Marsh."

"I'll let him know you're here." She motioned behind him. Ben walked over to the small sitting area. He'd have to fold his six-foot-three frame in half to fit in the tiny chairs. Instead, he walked to the refreshment bar and helped himself to a bottle of water.

On the other side of the tinted windows, cars cruised slowly down the street. A woman about his age pushed a stroller along the far sidewalk. No one noticed the county's greatest disappointment watching them through a plate-glass window.

"Ben."

He turned at the sound of his name. A gray-haired man in khakis and loafers walked toward him. Ben self-consciously straightened his tie. "Mr. Marsh. It's nice to finally meet you."

The older man took his hand and gave it a solid shake. "Thanks for being here. I'd show you around, but we have an appointment with Caroline Novak in my office. She's our training and event coordinator, and she's going to introduce you to our processes and help you get settled in."

Ben cringed. "I appreciate that, sir, but I don't need any special treatment."

John nodded as he led the way to a nearby elevator. "I know, and you're not getting it. All of our new employees are paired with a mentor. Caroline doesn't usually take on mentees, but you two knew each other growing up, so I thought it might be a good pairing." They stepped into the elevator, and John pressed the fourth-floor button.

They sort of knew each other. Ben tried to remember the last time he'd spoken to Caroline. Maybe when he and Chris graduated high school. He remembered her yelling at him and Chris for eating too much cake. Was that at his open house or Chris's?

The elevator doors opened to a lobby similar to the one downstairs. More blue and tan furniture with dark brown rugs covering parts of the tiled floor. Large windows offered a view of downtown. With few buildings standing more than four stories tall, Ben could see the rooftops of most of them.

John stepped off the elevator and turned right. Ben followed a step behind him. Only a handful of offices lined the hallway, all with window walls inside and out. Each office contained the same blue-and-brown striped carpet, tan walls, and oak furniture, but pictures, plants, and memorabilia gave each room a unique flair. They walked around the corner and into a fairly plain office. Pictures of John, his wife, and two sons covered the side table.

John motioned to one of two armchairs on the near side of the desk. "Caroline should be here soon. Until then, do you have any questions for me?"

Ben resisted the urge to loosen his tie as he sat. "I can't think of anything off the top of my head."

"Sorry I'm late. I hope you haven't been waiting long."

Caroline rushed into the office, her arms full of files and a smile on her face. A black skirt hugged her slender hips and legs, and she wore a light green, button-down shirt. He couldn't see all of her dark brown hair. Just the tight knot on the back of her head like she'd always worn it.

As she sat beside him, Ben checked his watch. It wasn't quite one o'clock. "I don't think you're late."

John laughed. "If Caroline isn't fifteen minutes early, she's late."

She set the files on the corner of John's desk and her purse on the floor. She turned, focusing on Ben. "Welcome home. I didn't realize until today you were back in town."

"ESPN isn't as interested in me selling insurance as they were when I was playing football." Neither were many people from his college life.

"I can't promise life here will be as exciting as you're used to, but you might attract some attention from the other employees."

"Which is why I asked Caroline to come out of retirement, if you will, to be your mentor." John leaned back in his chair. "Knowing your families' history, I thought it might be easier for you to work together without distractions. Caroline, do you have Ben's file there? I'd like to discuss some things with you both."

She grabbed the stack of files, flipping through the tabs. "I have it here someplace."

"Are those all of the other new employees?" Ben hadn't realized how many people worked at Morrison.

"No, most of these aren't even work related. Here it is." She pulled out a single file and passed it to John. He flipped to a page, then passed it back. Her face scrunched. "We don't have a Business Analytics department."

"I know," John said."

Caroline raised an eyebrow. "Are you letting Ben name his own position or just waiting until he finds something he likes?"

"What?" Ben stiffened. "Wasn't I hired as a business analyst?"

"I don't know. I didn't have a lot of time to review this." She practically glared at Ben. "I assume they hired you for your accounting minor."

Ben turned his attention to John. His temper simmered. "I know Al and my grandpa are friends, but I don't want special treatment." Like a made-up job for a washed-up ex-football player.

John lifted a hand. "Don't be too hasty. Your hiring wasn't standard, but it also wasn't an unmerited favor. You graduated with a three-point-eight GPA in business analytics while breaking and setting football records on the field at a division one university. You'd be an asset to any company, and Al wanted to make sure you didn't get away. You didn't get this job as a favor to you or your grandfather. It was a favor to us."

Confusion and embarrassment tied up his tongue. "I didn't realize …"

Cool fingers touched his hand. He looked at Caroline as she squeezed his arm. "You were always Chris's hardest working friend. That type of work ethic would be an asset anywhere."

Ben searched her blue eyes for any hint of patronization, but only sincerity looked back at him. Unsure what to say without embarrassing himself more, he nodded.

The corners of Caroline's mouth lifted.

For the first time all day, he relaxed.

"Would you mind giving John and me a minute?"

That couldn't be good.

Acknowledgements

I am ridiculously blessed and honored to work with and be inspired by so many amazing people in a profession that has the potential to be so isolating. I'd never survive alone on an island, and I can't thank these people enough for not making me try.

Tracy Donley and Jennifer Leo, my editors: thanks for making me look like a better writer than I really am.

LeAnne Bristow, my critique partner: your input and support motivate and encourage me. I hope I'm as helpful to you!

Pegg Thomas, my friend: your work as an editor is without question, but you've been my own personal cheerleader and shoulder to cry on/ear to vent to whenever I've needed one. You did it again this time—thank you.

Cheri Cowell and Rebecca Ford, my publishers: thanks for walking me through this. You took so much of the stress and anxiety out of this process. I probably could have figured this out eventually, but you helped me enjoy the experience.

Hannah Linder, my cover designer: you're simply amazing. Thank you for finding the perfect Jess.

Matty McMatt Matt: I can't think of anyone else who would let me call them such a ridiculous nickname, much less let me reveal it in a book. You are quite simply my most favoritest person in the whole world, and I couldn't do any of this without you.

I don't think I could possibly thank these people enough for their love, support, and correction—you all make me a better writer, but more importantly you make me a better person. Thank you.

And no acknowledgement page would be complete without recognizing my Lord and Savior for his work in my life. I recently recognized my novels for what they are: hopeful fiction with a healthy dose of romance. I didn't mean to write these kinds of stories, but I can't help myself. Jesus Christ *is* love, and the hope that I have in him cannot be matched. I just never realized how much it influences me until I saw it in my books.

About the Author

A writer and reader of hopeful fiction with a healthy dose of romance, Karin Beery can find the hope (and humor) in most any situation, including her marriage, her career, and her menagerie of fur babies who all insist on sleeping on her side of the bed. She enjoys kayaking, spending time with family and friends, and living in a Hallmark-ready smalltown.

A multi-award-winning author and editor with experience in traditional and self-publishing, freelance editing, and editing for publishers, when she's not writing, she runs Write Now Editing, helping authors turn good manuscripts into great books.

Stay connected and be the first to hear about new books, events, and other fun stories—scan here to sign up for her newsletter!